Copyright © 2024 Derek Heath.
All rights reserved.

Thank you for purchasing an authorised copy of this book. No part of this publication may be reproduced or redistributed without the prior written permission of the author.

"Green" first published in *The Old Ways: Volume Two* (2023) from Eerie River Press.

"Gold (My House is an Alligator)" first published (as "Diminishing Returns") in *Doors of Darkness* (2023) from TerrorCore Publishing.

Any references to historical events, real people, or real places are used fictitiously. Names, characters, and places are the products of the author's imagination.

First edition printed 2024 by Pope Lick Press.

DEREK HEATH

MARSH LIGHTS

STORIES

POPE LICK PRESS
2024

CONTENTS

Introduction 3

Pearl White 7
Ice Blue 37
Green 61
Blood Red 91
Gold (My House is an Alligator) 157
Coral 185
Amber 235

Also Available 268

Introduction

I've never introduced one of my books before. I'm not entirely sure that I've ever deemed one of my stories worthy of an introduction. Perhaps I figured it would be kinder not to waste any potential readers' time and just let them get straight into the horror; perhaps I'm just a little lazy. I'll let you decide.

Either way, I felt that *Marsh Lights* was the first of my books that has really deserved an introduction. Not necessarily because any of the stories within are any better than anything I've released so far, but because… well, I suppose because I feel they need the most explanation.

Every one of my books so far has represented a short period of my writing career; for example, if you're reading any one of my novellas, you can be fairly confident that it was written beginning-to-end, usually over one-to-three months. So what you're reading there is a snapshot – albeit a fairly overexposed and drawn-out snapshot – of a little block of my life.

My writing at that time will have been influenced by details of what's happening in my own life – sometimes, even the quality of the writing seems to have depended a little on when exactly the book was written. Even my first two short story collections, *Dark Nights* and *Dead Engines*, do much the same thing: every story in *Dark Nights* was written within a two-month period between writing chunks of my very first novella, *Day of the Mummy*, and *Dead Engines* was written in a week or so during a phase of very intense – and very specific and heightened – focus.

Why is this book different?

Marsh Lights is different – and very special to me – because it represents my entire career as a horror author. I've been writing for about half of my life now, and for most of that time, I've written horror. However, I only started publishing my books in early 2023 – almost a year and a half ago, as I write this – so most of my releases so far have been reflective of a time period within the last couple of years. What you're about to read, however, is a selection of stories from all over the place. One was written at the beginning of this year, and one in recent days. A couple were written between January and December 2023 (don't ask me exactly when) between other, larger works. "Blood Red" (under the working title "Plant Story" – I think I came up with that one on a particularly unimaginative night) was written at the end of 2019. *Amber* is one of the first horror stories I ever wrote, and was probably penned in 2017.

With a range of themes and a range of reflections on my life come a range of colours – hence the name of the book, and the 'colourful' names of the stories. I know that short story collections are always a risk – and especially one that ranges as much as this one hopes to. So please don't feel that you have to love every story. Just remember the ones you do, and know that I have put as much heart as I can into each one.

Without further ado, please enjoy the spectrum of horror that follows, and remember… we all change, all of the time. Be whatever colour you want to be.

Derek Heath
April 2024

PEARL

WHITE

JULY 25TH, 1916.

This physician was not the same one who'd amputated Damian's hand.

"Can you help me?" the boy slurred, his head lolling forward. The bandaged, throbbing stump of his left wrist lay heavily in his lap, hanging from his collar in a tattered sling. He was disturbingly malnourished, his khakis baggy in the middle. His neck was wet and red with blood, hair matted with sweat. He couldn't remember the last time he'd slept. "The dreams... can you help me with the dreams?"

"Patience," the physician said, his voice drifting across the medical tent as if through water. "I'm preparing the treatment for you now."

"I'm not going anywhere." Damian smiled exhaustedly. The twenty-year-old's tongue was thick, his stomach loose and squirming. "You got some morphine while you're at it, Doc?"

The doctor lurched across his view, momentarily blotting out the light of a single gas lamp. A loose flap billowed softly in the wind, a crude door painted white with a blood-red cross. The doctor was handed something from outside, then turned back to him. "No more painkillers," he said, his English clipped and awkward. "You will not assimilate correctly."

Damian swallowed. The physician's shape lingered before him for a second longer, a bleared silhouette with dark pits for eyes. Then it slipped away again, rummaging in another crate.

Through the film of blood in his eyes, Damian glimpsed a small shape wriggling in the specialist's hands. Like a fish, he thought groggily. Briefly he remembered the doctor poking two capsules into his mouth, his fingers thick and clammy.

"What did you give me?" Damian's own voice was funnelled toward his ears through a network of muddy pipes. He thought of Eric.

The old man exploded into view again, leering into the boy's face. Examining him. "Are you ready, boy?"

Damian squinted, focusing hard. "Ready?"

The doctor's eyes were jaundiced, his nose sharp and bruised. His flesh was sprayed white in patches, his left cheek and threads of his wrinkled neck ghostly pale. Thin, grey hair was oiled back from a cracked forehead, patterned with the same pure-white blotches.

"Boy," the doctor snapped, clicking his fingers.

Damian's head rolled forward and he realised it had been slowly tipping back. He was drooling. "Are you ready to begin the process?"

Damian looked down. The old man was gripping something, a brown shape the size of a small kit bag. "This will help? With the dreams?"

"Oh, yes," the doctor smiled thinly. His accent was sharp, deliberately crafted to erase traces of an accent that Damian might have been able to place, were he more lucid. Ethanol blossomed stiffly on the old man's breath. "You won't dream anymore."

The physician's nubby fingers were curled into loose hooks around its edges of the thing. Its shape was familiar, though it was different somehow.

"It's German," the young man slurred. His legs were numb. His left hand, amputated months ago after a chunk of shrapnel had threatened infection, seemed to ache and thrum as if still attached. "Why's it German?"

"Why waste Ally resources?" the doctor shrugged.

Damian's good right hand dangled limply by his side. His eyes were threaded with blood, cheeks sallow and stubbled. Deep, thick frown lines had appeared on his forehead when the nightmares had begun and hadn't gone away again. Eric had laughed and told him that, when they returned home, he would look like his father. Damian had grinned and said that his father was out here somewhere, too, perhaps not on the Somme but in the country at least. His own wrinkles would be twice as deep when the war was finally over.

"How long do I wear it?"

"Not long."

"Okay."

"You are ready?"

Damian's eyes returned to the thing in the doctor's hands. His chest fluttered hesitantly.

The gas mask seemed to be watching him, its creamy celluloid lenses splintered by the legs of the metal 'spiders' locked into their circular frames. The leather was brown and oily, the filter unit a bulky canister hanging loosely from its chin.

He had been assured that the technology applied to the mask was cutting-edge.

"I don't want to see their faces anymore," Damian whispered as the doctor stood up, looming over him. "That's all. The screams... I don't want to hear them."

"You won't," said the old man. He inverted the mask, presenting Damian with the inside. His fingers were hooked into the lacquer seam lining the edge of the mask. "It is time."

Damian's eyes widened.

The interior mesh wriggled hungrily, the celluloid circles of the eyes flaring with the greasy light of the gas lamp. Damian tried to recoil from the mask as it was raised toward his face, but his body was paralysed, legs and arms pumped full of lead. He tried to speak;

couldn't.

Thin, wormy protrusions bucked and reared out of the leather mesh, some as long as his thumb. Tiny pointed teeth flashed, hooks and barbs exploding from tapered heads no larger than the point of a pin. They writhed violently, snapping hungrily at his face. Damian's breathing was suddenly heavy, his heart smacking the walls of his chest. He might be imagining the tiny worm-like things. Christ, at this point, he could have been hallucinating the doctor.

The mask was lifted closer to him and he swallowed. Closer. Closer. No, they were real, definitely real, he could hear them *hissing*—

"No," he managed finally. "No, don't—"

The mask snapped onto his face. Hundreds of mouths latched to his skin, needle-like teeth burrowing immediately into the flesh. The papery straps connected behind his head, the doctor's hands working quickly. The leather was hot and wet. He smelled blood.

He couldn't breathe. The canister bounced against his neck as he struggled against the buckles. Thick blooms of heat punched into his lungs.

He screamed as the suckling mouths ripped into his pores, his agonised shrieks muffled through the canister. His whole body bucked and writhed in the chair.

"Like I say," the doctor smiled, a blur of movement

through the celluloid lenses, "you will not wear it for long."

He wasn't bothering to disguise his accent anymore.

"It wears you now."

Damian yowled, suffocating, as something wriggled into his ear and bit into the tissue of his brain – then a thick, deep cold spread through his entire body, like icy water flooding an empty vessel.

SEPTEMBER 1ST, 1916.

The sky was white as bone, scalloped by the clawing fingers of titanic beech boughs. These had begun to bristle gold and blood-red as the last of the summer heat withdrew and the chill of a French winter seeped into the ground. Broader hornbeam branches formed a thick canopy, still thick with bright green leaves, their trunks shadowy in the miasmic, rolling fog. Twisted knots of hazel formed spindly webs, connecting the larger trees, gnarled black worms trembling at the edges of the clearing.

Mist rolled over the top of the trench – a gummy black grin, carved violently through the clearing – forming a cloud-like ceiling over the troops huddled inside. The muck down there was saturated, forming wrinkled bulwarks either side of the hunched bodies pressed together; fallen leaves drifted through the fog occasionally, joining others in puddles of accumulated moisture on the trench floor.

Far from the woods, the Somme rumbled with detonations of gunfire.

Eric shuddered, his back pressed hard to the wall of cold, compact dirt. He had removed his old Brodie helmet and he gripped it in both hands, boots planted firmly in the earth. His hair was buzzed short around his ears and the back of his skull, but thick tangles of brown drooped from his forehead into his closed eyes. His cheeks were blistered with caked mud and sweat. A Lee-Enfield rifle stood on its butt between his knees, the barrel resting on his padded shoulder.

"Can't do it," he breathed. "Can't do it, can't do it, can't…"

They had been trapped down here for days now. German artillery would mow them down if they tried to escape the salient that the village and woods had formed; some had tried.

There were half a dozen men in the clearing. The carcasses of seven more had been dragged into the trench from the forest floor; it seemed more dignified to keep them down here, though they had been turned onto their fronts and covered with blankets.

One of the men nudged Eric in the ribs. He looked up as Private Tilley offered him a slimy water canteen. Tilley's face had been burned so badly that the right eye was wedged shut; his hands trembled, filth caked into the nails. Eric smiled a polite refusal, twisting his helmet in his hands.

Tilley thrust the canteen, his eyes hard. "Take it," he insisted.

Resigned, Eric took the canteen. He unscrewed the cap and drank, grimacing as the stale water slid down his throat.

"You good?" Tilley said quietly as Eric handed back the flask. It had been weeks since Damian had disappeared. Months, maybe. Didn't matter.

"I'm good, Tilley," Eric lied, peering into the trench. Asleep beneath a crude blanket of sodden jackets, Private Newton muttered some half-intelligible line from an Al Jolson song and rolled onto his side, chin gouging his filthy collar. Two Pinochle-playing privates quietly smoked damp cigarettes, their movements as subdued and dull as those of a pair of clockwork figurines. Behind them, Stallard drew sludgy shapes in the trench floor with a broken branch. He was enormous and quiet, his shoulders massive caps on the barrel of his chest.

Tilley clapped a big hand on Eric's shoulder and squeezed kindly before stretching to kick Newton in the ribs with the toe of his boot. As the seventeen-year-old's eyes opened and he rolled over blearily, Tilley offered him the canteen.

Eric turned, gazing down the trench at the bodies

laid in the dirt, indistinguishable from each other beneath the blankets. Just lumps. Sergeant Quaid was in there somewhere. Four or five men that Eric had known well. He wondered if their families would ever know what had happened here.

He remembered Damian and his chest shuddered. He swallowed sobs. Wouldn't do to let the others see him cry. Not again.

"Can't do it," he whispered. Behind him, Newton was drizzling water into his mouth. "Can't do it. Can't do it…"

A swathe of blackness crossed his vision, then disappeared. A shadow slipping through the trench, or the fleeting vestige of a short burst of sleep? Then he was awake, and Brian Stallard crouched before him, the older man's eyes bright and shining despite the colourlessness of his face. "We're going over," he said gruffly. "Last chance, Eric. We can take them."

"Can't—"

"Don't give me that shit. We're here for a reason, kid. Want to help us out?"

"Sergeant's dead. They're all dead, Bri. We can't—"

"We can, and we will." Stallard nodded grimly. "They've got the village, Toulson. We need to get it back."

Eric swallowed. He stared at the rifle for a while, then nodded up at the private who'd resigned himself to their late sergeant's responsibilities. "All right," he said. The fog rolled quietly above them. "Up and over. Why not."

JULY 14TH.

"What did he tell you?" Damian whispered, nudging Eric in the ribs with his good arm. Occasionally there came a rattling burst from the Lewis as it ripped a fan of fire and smoke through the dewy haze above them. The Somme was a scarred mess of broken earth around them; Delville Wood was a smudge of insignificant grey on the horizon. "Come on, you know I'm not gonna spill anything. Me and you, we're *great* at secrets."

Eric smiled, though his lips were tight. "You think half the men down here don't know about us?"

Damian grinned. "They don't care. I don't care. But you can't start keeping secrets from me, now, can you?"

The machine-gun fired again, great plumes of greasy power rocketing from the dirt above them. Stallard was on firing duty at the moment, though it had taken all three of them to build the gun quickly. The big man yelled as he squeezed the trigger, pumping out ten rounds of ammunition every second in five-second bursts. The battlefield above their heads trembled with frequent mortar explosions and hunks of mud and debris filtered down onto their shoulders and chests. Eric clung to his Lee-Enfield, knowing that at any moment they'd be called up top and dreading it. He was never afraid, never happy, never melancholic or distracted. The only feeling that registered now was dread. It was all that was left. A permanent state of being.

Damian poked him again, this time with the butt of his standard-issue Webley. Damian preferred the rifle, but since the explosion that had cost him his hand, that choice had been removed from him. One-handed, he had decided he would rather return to the Mk VI revolver than return home. Eric admired him for that. He often wished Damian would see sense and request transport to a casualty clearing station; from there he would no doubt be taken to a hospital away from the front for proper care. Maybe Eric could join him out there, if he asked Stallard to swing the Lewis around and spend a few rounds of ammunition ripping off his leg.

"Hey," Damian was saying. "Hey, where've you gone? Look at me."

He saw the red rings of Damian's eyes, the thick grey bags beneath. They never slept at the same time; they had decided weeks ago that if one of them were asleep, the other would keep watch. This meant that

Eric was the only soldier who knew just how badly Damian was suffering. Oh, they all saw terrible things when they closed their eyes, but Damian slept as if his entire body were aflame. Much of the time he was awake he would drift off or fall into a seizure, his eyes rheumy and vacant, his chest heaving.

"Sorry," Eric shook his head. "Somewhere else."

"You wish," Damian muttered, one-handedly tucking the revolver away. "So tell me, then. What's the plan?"

Eric tipped his head back and smiled thinly up at the sky. It was on fire. Always on fire. "I can't," he said. "If I tell anyone anything, Haig'll kill me. You know how precious he is about his plans."

"Well, fair enough," Damian shrugged, "but who am I going to tell? Look, if you get to be all pally with the general, I reckon you ought to tell your only friend what he's got planned for us before we both die out here."

"What's this? Did I say something?"

"No," Eric said quietly. "No, you're just… beautiful."

Damian said something in return, but a booming swell of machine-gun fire inches from them meant that Eric didn't catch a word. For a moment the trench was alight with the bright greasy firework-flares of the Lewis, then it was dark again.

"Haig didn't really tell me anything," Eric lied,

turning his head away. It was easier than trying to explain why he couldn't tell Damian what the general was planning. That even though Eric trusted him more than anything, Haig would probably shoot them both if he caught even a whiff that Eric had spilled. He had confided in the young private in confidence, in a strange moment of self-doubt. It didn't mean Haig and Eric were friends. Eric had just been in the right place at the right time. "He basically just said we're probably going to be out here awhile."

This much was true. General Haig hadn't taken his plans to the War Committee yet, but he was optimistic. Pressure, that was the plan. Haig was going to advocate that they keep pushing against the German armies in France for as long as they could. He thought they'd have enough tanks by mid-September for an attack he was planning with the French; by then, he believed the German defence would be weak enough that one final affront would gain the Allies a titanic advantage.

This advantage, Haig was certain, would be monumental in bringing about the end of the war.

"Well, then," Damian said, slouching back against the trench wall and fumbling for a cigarette, "I guess we'd better settle in for a few more restless nights."

***

SEPTEMBER 1ST.

The six of them emerged from the fog, dark and filthy silhouettes climbing slowly out of the trench like exhausted demons finally escaping Hell. All six carried Lee-Enfield rifles across their waists. They rose to different heights, none of them entirely able to stand straight, all of them caked in blood and earth.

Stallard turned to his men and nodded, his Brodie helmet bobbing a little on his head. No longer were these helmets a commodity; still, finding one that was exactly the right size was difficult. His face was grim and shadowy, bright eyes flaring like silver pennies in the fog. "We take the village," he said firmly. Around them the trees were still and silent, watchful sentinels holding fast against the soft, chilled wind. "They've been quiet the last couple days. We're outnumbered, boys, but if we go quietly—"

"We can do it," Eric nodded, suddenly sure. He gripped his rifle tight, hands cold, the fingers stiff. He gazed ahead into the trees. Distantly he heard gunfire, continuous and terrible; occasionally an explosion of heavier sound punctuated the soundscape which, otherwise, had become as commonplace as silence.

"Good boy."

The six of them stood there for a moment, teetering on the edge of Hell, barely a yard from the trench that had become home, up to their waists in rolling fog.

"Alby, Hank"—here he looked toward the two soldiers who had been playing cards—"take the church, then you can keep us covered from the tower."

"Got you, boss," Alby said quietly, checking his rifle. Hank nodded grimly beside him.

"Newt, you're with me. We'll head around to the right."

Bill Newton nodded, his eyes wide and alert, his face red and feverish.

"Eric, Jim—"

Crack.

Stallard froze, his eyes darting to the edge of the clearing. Immediately Eric raised his rifle, pointing the heavy thing into the trees and squinting down the barrel.

For a full minute there was thick, dreadful silence.

Then footfalls. Suddenly all around them, heavy and careless. Boots dragging over dry earth, branches snapping and cracking and breaking as dozens of figures came through the trees around them.

"*Retreat,*" Stallard whispered, but it was too late.

The fog was ripped open as the first shot barrelled into the trees and into nothing. Alby reloaded loudly as the others raised their own rifles. Eric's head pounded frantically as he swung his weapon left and right, staring into the forest as shadows began to lengthen and separate. The shapes shuffled forward, boots dragging in the dirt, and Eric took a stumbling step back.

"What…"

Points of yellow light flared from the trees, reflections of sunlight in glassy lenses. Eric heard frightened mumbling behind him; another shot exploded right next to his ear.

A ring of hazy shapes surrounded them, figures silhouetted in the mist. Reaching, clawing at the air as they emerged from the trees. Eric swung his body around and saw with horror that they had approached from every side, every angle, that there were still more of them coming. Retreat was impossible: where could they go but back into the trench? The only option was—

"Fire!" Stallard yelled, raising his rifle and squeezing the trigger.

The Lee-Enfield pumped a streak of grey into one of the nearest figures and its stomach erupted into a spray of black ichor. Eric's eyes widened as the silhouette looked down

(*his head's the wrong shape*)

at the gaping hole in its midsection, then looked up again. Behind him another shot, and then another, and then the clearing was a haze of gunsmoke and fire and screaming and he joined them, why not, swinging his rifle toward the next silhouette and firing.

He caught the silhouette in the neck and its body twitched, yellow eyes swinging as its head bucked. It lurched forward, shuffling in heavy, black boots. Its head was bulbous and awful, the throat bulging where a squarish protrusion swung from its chin. The eyes were enormous and smeared with soot. Eric reloaded, fired again, this time for a figure the other side of the clearing. Yelling, the others pumped shots into the trees, the clearing suddenly ripped open by gunfire. One figure doubled over as a bullet smacked it squarely in the kneecap, but instead of falling to the floor it shuffled on, body crooked over.

"They're not going down!" Hank yelled somewhere behind him. Eric fumbled with the chamber, slamming another bullet into the rifle and lifting it again. This time he aimed for the silhouette's awful, misshapen tumour of a head—

Gas masks.

They were all wearing gas masks.

He paused. Only for a second, but long enough to clock at least thirty men approaching from the far side of the clearing. Behind him he knew there must be thirty more.

"Gas attack!" Stallard yelled.

Eric fired, ripping open the head of the figure with the busted kneecap. The gas mask exploded, lenses shattering, and the silhouette finally crumpled. It sprawled on the floor, squirming uselessly. There was something wrong here. Something awfully, dreadfully wrong.

Dread.

It was all he'd felt for months. But never stronger than this. In his ear another deafening explosion of sound. A scream. "What do we do?"

He raised his rifle and locked onto another figure's head. The blank, disc-like eyes of the gas mask were focused on him. He fired. The bullet sailed pointlessly into the mist. Another explosion by his shoulder. He looked desperately at Stallard and the big man looked back.

"They're unarmed," he whispered.

It was true. They were closing in on the trench now, marching purposefully forward: a small army of empty-handed men.

"Gas—" Stallard started, but Eric shook his head.

"The fog!" he yelled, turning his head and pumping another shot into the chest of one of the approaching figures. "The wind's blowing it toward the village!"

Stallard nodded, reloading. If this were a gas attack, it was very poorly timed. The Germans would only be poisoning their home base. Beside him James Tilley stumbled back as he fired off a shot, smashing a glassy yellow eye with a well-discharged bullet. Something wrong, he thought, something else—

The uniforms, he realised.

British uniforms.

"Stop firing!" Eric yelled, wheeling around again. "They're our men! They're our—"

Alby screamed as one of the figures lurched forward suddenly, thrusting a hand out and clamping its gloved fingers around his neck. The rifle dropped uselessly from Alby's hands as the figure butted its masked head into his, the lenses smashing into his forehead and shattering against bone. His head shot back and the figure twisted its wrist, crushing his throat. The scream died in Alby's throat and he dropped to the floor.

The silhouette turned its head toward Eric and he saw, through the ragged lens frames, an empty void of shadow. No, not empty…

There was something wriggling in there.

"What in Hell—"

The figure reached down and grabbed Alby's abandoned rifle. Before any of the others could react it had straightened up and thrust the weapon into the meat of Hank's stomach.

Eric saw Hank's organs fan out from his back in a greasy spray of black and red before he heard the shot. The slimy fountain of ichor was followed by a colossal thundercrack, then Hank fell to his knees and began to sway.

Around them, the clearing imploded.

The soft pulp of Eric's brain smashed into the back of his skull as his head hit the floor. His eardrums vibrated, gunfire filling his head, his jaws tight with agony. He screamed as his right ear was pumped full of blood, thunder cracking just west of his right eyeball, lightning flashing even closer.

Eyes rolling upward, he saw the bone-white sky through a film of glossy red. There was another titanic *bang!* and a thick weight fell onto his legs. Boots champed into the ground around him, shuffling figures barrelling past. He looked up and saw blank celluloid eyes gazing down at him, hollow of emotion. Tilley lay still across his legs.

Eric screamed as Stallard's eyes were blown out of his head, pink billowing into the fog from a ragged hole at the base of his skull. Something had grabbed Eric's arm and was trying to drag him backward. He struggled against the thick-fingered grip, fumbling for something, anything, and found a knife tucked into his belt. Withdrew it quickly, thrust it upward—

The blade sank into his attacker's thigh and sheared past bone, sliding into a tight knot of meat. The attacker tightened its grip on his arm, unfazed. Eric yanked the knife back and the blade came out sticky and black, tiny leech-like things squalling in the blood.

A boot slammed down on his wrist and smashed it into the ground with a sickening *crunch*. The blade fell from his hand and a yellow lens flashed close to his face. Newton's body hit the ground, inches from him, and he shrieked. In the corner of his eye he saw a black-gloved hand reach into Newton's throat and rip it out.

A glimpse of bandage, fluttering in the wind.

He struggled onto his front, tried to stagger to his feet but crashed into another figure, looking blankly down at him. The celluloid was cracked; minute shapes writhed behind the lens.

"What are—"

The butt of a rifle – *his* rifle – smashed into the back of his head and the fog turned black and swallowed him whole.

Eric caught flashes: jawbone smashing into the dirt as he was dragged along; legs, numb and heavy behind him; a one-armed figure leading the march as others dragged him out of the trees and toward the village.

The church loomed out of the enfolded crystal and smoke that made up the sky. The earth was ripe with the smell of death. He drifted again, slipping into the dark.

Damian...

When he snapped awake he was sitting upright, head tipped back. He gazed into the church rafters, every beam drooling with shadow. He vaguely sensed movement in spangles of faraway light. His hands were bound tightly behind his back, crushed between his spine and the hard, vertical back of the church pew. Others lay broken and burned around him, scattered and overturned across the nave. He peered through the dust and his eyes settled on the presbytery.

A hunched figure in a gas mask gazed blankly back at him. It stood awkwardly, one of its legs bent slightly inward, the British uniform it wore punched through with holes. There were other figures in the church, one or two standing so deep in the shadows that all Eric could make out were the yellowy discs of their eyes. The fruity death-smell was stronger here. He looked into the eyes of the masked figure in the presbytery. The grey-green filtration canister bobbed as it breathed.

Its left hand was missing.

"Damian…" Eric breathed. "What is this? I thought you'd *died*, man, I thought…"

The one-armed thing just stared. It had to be him. Must have been. Tufts of stiff black hair poked up around the straps of the gas mask. He was the same height, same build, and his arm…

"Why are you wearing that?" Eric said.

The figure stepped forward, rubber heel clapping the stone flags. Its stare was empty and terrifying.

"Damian. It's me, it's Eric. Please…"

The Damian-thing raised its good hand and gestured. A figure swung out of the shadows toward them. The body was different, but the mask was the same. German. Brown leather. Metal-legged 'spiders' in its eyes. The uniform was French: the blue tunic was splashed with blood and tiny flecks of bone. No boots;

the thing shuffled barefoot, toes curled into claws.

Eric wriggled in his seat, dismayed to learn that his ankles were bound too. His Webley revolver pressed tightly against his side, but it was useless there. The thing staggered toward him and for half a second the filtered sunlight flared in its eyes and they burned like stars—

The figure stopped. The Damian-thing tipped its head back and made a strange, insect-like clicking sound. The sound was muffled and corrupted by the respirator but still deafeningly loud and unnatural.

"What's going on?" Eric breathed. "Why…"

The Damian-thing turned its masked head to gaze unwaveringly at him. The bloody Frenchman did the same.

"What—"

The French soldier lifted both hands to the side of its head, grabbed the gas mask by two folds of spare leather, and *ripped*.

Eric yelled as wings of black viscera sprayed the Frenchman's chest. Another rattling, clicking sound, coming from the French soldier this time: a roiling screech of sheer agony. The soldier fell to his knees, sagging forward as the mask released its terrible grip on his face. Thrashing tails writhed inside the thing as it dropped wetly to the floor. The man swayed on his knees for a moment, face sloughed off to leave a charred, black plate of bone. Runnels of ink drooled down his neck and into his tunic and finally, heavily, he toppled. The sound boomed into the church.

The Damian-thing reached down to pick up the mask, still wriggling. The insides of the lenses were wet with black gunk, the worm-like things fused to the leather snapping and biting.

"Damian, please, I don't know what this is but you don't have to – no, stay back, please—"

He bucked his wrists, struggling to loosen the knotted rope behind him. Wriggling in the pew, he kept his eyes on the mask as Damian stepped toward him.

"Please. This isn't you, I know it isn't." His eyes flitted from the writhing mask to the one knitted to Damian's face and back again. "Damian, get *away* from me—"

His wrist snapped loudly and he yelped, pushing through the pain to try and work his hands free. He slammed his ankles against the pew, heart pounding as Damian advanced on him, holding the mask aloft…

"You're not putting that thing on me," Eric grunted. "Stop this, Damian, stop it – *think*…"

But he couldn't, Eric realised. Not independently, not anymore.

"Look, I don't know what they did to you," he sobbed desperately, "but if this thing is controlling you – those… *leeches* – if they're in your head… Damian, you have to fight them. Please. Whatever they're telling you to do – is it the Germans? Did the Germans do this to you? – look, Damian, whatever that *fucking mask* is making you do, you don't have to—"

Damian stepped closer, thrusting the empty mask forward with his good hand. Tiny teeth snapped in chittering gums.

(*it's not Damian anymore*)

That much was obvious.

(*so why does it want* you?)

He was under the mask's control, *German* control—

"Not just control," Eric breathed, bucking his whole body to try and rip his fists out of their bonds. The pew rocked and he shook his head, laughed bitterly, madly. "It's in your head. It knows what you know…"

But what Damian knew wasn't enough.

(*what do* you *know?*)

The leeches had seen inside Damian's mind.

A memory:

(*if I tell anyone, Haig'll kill me. You know how precious he is about his plans*)

"Oh god," Eric whispered.

The knot loosened.

The mask snapped at his face and he ducked, rolling off the pew and ripping his hands apart with a scream. The Damian-thing wheeled after him, an insect-shriek of clicks and whistles detonating inside its mask. Eric staggered blindly into the nave, tripping over the ropes around his ankles. He tumbled onto his stomach, grabbing madly for the next pew, one hand slipping inside his jacket—

"I'm sorry," he whispered, locking his fingers around the Webley. Movement behind him: another of the masked figures shuffling in his direction. More rattling, louder this time – what was that, a call to arms?

They have the village.

Tears ran down his face and Eric withdrew the revolver, thumbing down the hammer.

Mid-September. That was when Haig stopped putting pressure on the Germans and started putting the *fight* to them. That was when everything changed. And if he gave them that...

Leeches snapped their hooked teeth inches from Eric's face and he jammed the revolver into the soft flesh of his chin. Looking up into Damian's face, he saw only the vacant celluloid eyes of the thing that had consumed him. The metal legs of the 'spiders' clamped inside the frames, their spindly bodies bleary and ghost-like.

"I'm sorry," he whispered again. "I'm sorry, Damian. I hope the dreams have stopped."

The first leeches snapped onto his cheeks and he screamed, pumping the trigger before they could start drilling into his flesh. A single round smashed through the centre of Eric's skull and smeared his brains on the stone flags, and his body fell limply to the floor.

Author's Note:

I remember three things very clearly about writing this story. The first is that I was listening to the soundtrack for John Carpenter's The Fog *on repeat, and had it eerily creeping into my ears for the entire time I was writing; I've often wondered how different the story would have been if I had been writing in silence, like I usually do. The second is that no matter how much research I did – this story was set during the first world war, if you couldn't tell, which I did not experience or live through (obviously) and felt deserved as much truth as I could inject – I still felt I was getting so many things wrong. I apologise for any mistakes or anachronisms. I think they'll come back to haunt me. The third thing is that I was horrendously ill and stuck in bed, and had to elbow my way through a mountain of tissues to reach the keyboard. Did you enjoy it? Good luck ever enjoying it again, with that image in mind.*

ICE BLUE

1

My legs buckled beneath me as I lurched back onto the *Hexenspinne*, bringing with me a few gallons of ice and a new albatross.

Which was heavier, I could not say.

I felt that the old fishmonger had suspected me of something; perhaps he knew of my strange catch, had heard some rumour on the salt and the stiff ocean wind. Perhaps he could smell the queer toxin of guilt on my breath, the terror reeking on my week-old clothes, sense the unease sitting in my stomach like a sick man waiting to die. I knew I must look weary, my hair unwashed and tangled, my oilskin sodden. I wondered how deep the sallow pits around my eyes had become. But the way he had looked at me…

Perhaps he had simply wanted more for the ice.

The deck of my tiny yawl was slick with saltwater and blood. A fine red spray decorated the pedestal of the wheel, glittering in the dusk-light. I had brought aboard a few dozen cod on my most recent trip around the dogger bank, and many had flopped onto the deck still alive and twitching. The fine copper mist swilling in the water was a dreadful reminder of the great numbers of tiny heads I had flattened with my old priest. Quickly I loosed my mooring ropes, turning out to sea before the fishmonger could come out of his hut.

The ocean was unusually calm, points of white punctuating every softly-swelling wave. A blanket of mist rolled across the surface, stained a creamy pink by the fading sunlight. I gripped the wheel with hands that only stopped trembling when I squeezed the life from the thick, oak handles; my knuckles bulged so violently I thought they might break skin.

When I was a way from the harbour, I staggered away from the wheel and went to the barrels. Usually I kept fish in them, packed tightly with straw. Before I had docked, I had emptied one of the barrels and heaved my queer find into it, folding the thing over itself so that it would fit. The cod I had released into the ocean watched me from the churning surface as I did so, their cold black eyes tiny points of judgement in the dark. They bobbed silently, mouths agape, clumps of straw floating in the foam between their bodies. I had saved a little straw and covered the top of the keg. Now it stunk – ripely, colourfully – of putrefaction.

Digging my arms reluctantly into the barrel, I

removed all the straw I could. A few scales came too, ripping thin runnels of blood from my wrists. The thing inside the barrel watched me with cold black eyes of its own; gingerly, I reached down with my thumb and index finger to close the lids. They almost clicked into place, so brittle was the flesh.

I poured ice around the thing, filling every space, packing its folded limbs tight. When I had shaken the keg to make sure some ice fell to the bottom, I packed in more. More still, until only the thing's face was visible. This I stared at for some time.

It was impossible, that face. Not just frightening, but impossible.

More ice, until it was covered. Even then I kept filling the barrel. Shaking it so pieces filtered down, spangles of blue tumbling upward through the glassy debris. More. When the chunks were packed together tightly enough, they became a filter of crystalline white; when more layers were piled on top, it might have been possible to forget that the shadowy shape in the barrel even *had* a face.

Possible, but not easy.

2

Less than twenty-four hours previous, I discovered the creature.

From all sides thick blossoms of fog batted my

yawl, waves of it punching the deck with thick knots of ocean spray. The rain was horrendous and had been chasing me for hours in the belly of a titanic black cloud which, now, had detonated and filled the whole sky. The moon was gone, the only reminder of its presence a lambent glow in the fog. I screamed as I pressed my body against the wheel, the kegs sliding about behind me. I could not tell you now what I was screaming, but the words drove my throat entirely hoarse.

It was impossible to see through the fog and the spray, but I pushed the yawl forward nonetheless. I had a vague sense of my bearings – or thought I did – and thought myself close enough to harbour that I'd have a good enough chance of spotting the beam of the lighthouse.

I yowled as a thick pillar of stone plunged out of the fog before my boat, nearly skewering the bow. Pummelling the wheel, I managed to pull the yawl to port, narrowly skirting the stony needle. It was gone before I could fully register its size, but I was confident that at least this meant I was closing in on shore.

So where was the lighthouse?

I had no time to explore the possibilities. I shrieked as another rock, just as tall and sharp as the first, smashed into the hull and rent the outer panels with a great wet shredding of wood. The sound was like that of breaking bone and I yanked the wheel hard to starboard, diving into the fog and almost tipping the boat over. I tumbled away from the wheel, scrambling desperately to pull down the sails. My hands were sore and frozen, the ropes sodden and thick and thrashing like tentacles.

My eyes widened as a crown of rocks thrust out of the ocean, a set of gnarled black teeth in the foggy mouth yawing open before me. A belt of impossibly tall stone needles rising from the mist, keening forward as though reaching for the hull—

3

After a fitful and brief rest, I checked on the barrel.

The ice was beginning to thaw, not so much that it had yet liquefied, but enough that the chalky white texture was lost; smoother now, less crystalline and more transparent, the top layer had been welded into a nobbled lens so that I could see more clearly the thing inside the keg. I swallowed, gripping the sides of the barrel with white knuckles as I gazed down into it. Behind me, tied to the mizzen as always, was the good luck charm I had inherited from my father: a whaling harpoon, for years unused. He had hoped I would follow in his footsteps, but of course the whales were all gone. Nonetheless the harpoon had come with me on every voyage, an heirloom which I had vowed to make use of should the opportunity ever present. The

Hexenspinne was not nearly large enough to carry a whale carcass to shore, and I doubted I had the necessary skills to slay one; regardless, I had vowed.

Now I considered plunging the harpoon into the belly of the thing in the barrel and tossing it overboard. It was dead, I was sure; it had no heartbeat.

But still…

The creature watched me back, its eyes bright blue points beneath the ice. Its face was in shadow but the features had clarified a little, bleary through the lumps in its slowly-thawing encasement. Its flesh was pale, the malnourished body a twisted knot of white-pink beneath the shape of the head. I had been forced to break one of its limbs to get it into the keg; a bony knee pressed into the side of the container, poking out at an odd angle.

I stepped away from the barrel, satisfied that the ice would last, at least, till I sailed the *Hexenspinne* to port again.

Hadn't I closed its eyes?

I stood frozen for a moment, halfway to the wheel. The deck of the yawl swayed beneath me as the ocean churned, slopping weakly onto the rails. My heart, too, had stopped in my chest. The sea was calm but I was reminded of that night: the thick, yellow fog, miasmic and gloomy and choking and ghastly; the dreadful, keening rocks; the place beyond. Those tiny blue points bore into me, the barrel at my back but that unflinching, cold stare drilling into my mind. The image of the thing's face was hooked into the roof of my mouth and made me nauseous. I could only swallow it.

Hadn't I closed them?

I couldn't be sure. It didn't matter. Either way, I knew there was only one thing I could do. Should do.

Throw it back, whispered the voice in my head. *Throw it into the ocean.*

I should have. But, god help me... you'd understand. If you'd seen those eyes – if you'd seen its face – you'd understand why I couldn't do that.

4

I remember thinking my heart was going to fall out of my mouth.

Rocks lurched at me from the fog and I battled with the wheel, keening the yawl through a belt of tall black needles. I was screaming, my throat hoarse and dry, my skin saturated by the constant barrage of salt-water but my insides on fire as thick bolts of adrenaline pumped through my body. Another pillar of stone leered up at port, scraping the side of the boat with a dreadful moaning cry, and I yanked the wheel to starboard, tugging it sharply back before another cluster of rocks dashed the hull. Water smashed the mast and it swung, forcing me to duck my head; when I lifted my eyes I saw a crown of black thorns punching up from the waves directly ahead of the yawl and turned hard to port—

The *Hexenspinne* surged through a bank of foamy water and smacked the surface as it fell, so hard I was shaken from the wheel. Stumbling back to it I prepared to dodge more rocks, swinging my eyes left and right to see which strip of ocean would assault me next.

The sail billowed softly behind me. The sea was strangely calm, almost flat; the rocks were gone.

Quickly I pulled down the sail and threw anchor. Behind the yawl, tall dark points had become blurry silhouettes in the roiling fog. Waves crashed onto the stones and splashed the flat water my side of the rock belt; I was encircled by the dark pillars, but momentarily – so I thought, at least – safe.

Taking a breath, I finally staggered to the rails and looked to bow. The boat bobbed gently. The fog was thinner, the wind still.

Totally still.

I was in a clearing of sorts, the only sound the punching of the waves behind me, muffled by moist walls of mist.

An intense relief flooded my body and I pushed wet hair out of my eyes, peering into the fog to see if I could spy an opening in the rocks that surrounded my little oasis. I could only see more dark shapes; the only way out of the clearing would be through them. Well, then, I thought, I would simply wait for the weather outside of this queer little vortex to calm down. I had made it in, so I could surely make it out again.

But how tall must these rocks be, to break the surface this far from harbour? The water must be half a mile deep out here. More, maybe.

Eventually I looked down.

I had been somewhat conscious of the shapes bobbing around the yawl, but through the fog and a filter of panic I had not drawn any conclusions, nor spared them an appropriate amount of attention. A film of mist drifted across the surface, so that I might have been anchored in a bank of cloud. Beneath this yellowish skin the water itself was black.

"Dear god," I whispered. I remember not what I said afterward.

I think I may have simply moaned in horror as I looked over the edge, regrettably transfixed by the pale shapes floating on the surface.

5

The horizon was a knife edge, the blade heated and curved and pressed to the ball of the ocean so that you could feel it burning the blue skin; the rising sun scraped itself on sharp steel as it heaved itself from the depths, leaking sulphurous yellow into banks of cloud and spraying the water with heat. Flaying itself. I watched its lurid display as I piloted the yawl toward the next dogger bank, eyeing a series of dark points in the distance that I knew were larger fishing vessels. The way the birds circled them, darting to the surface occasionally to snatch a flash of silver from the waves, told me that there were fish to be had here.

The water was calm as we scythed forward, the deck slowly drying in the morning sun. I had kept myself below deck overnight, and the frost that had gathered on the handles of the wheel and the railings was almost fully thawed. The sail clapped quietly behind me. I was supplied an opportunity to forget my strange catch, to forget the treacherous rock belt and the salt-water clearing beyond. To forget what I had brought aboard. I was simply at one with the *Hexenspinne*, as I had so often been, controlling the wheel not with my hands but with electrical impulses, with instinct. We worked together, following the path the sea offered, guiding each other gently forward. This was how it should have been. How it had always been. The yawl and I were perfect together. I think I may have allowed myself to smile.

We were halfway to the dogger bank when something thumped the hull from beneath, a heavy head butting the bottom of the boat so violently the boom skewed forward and smashed into the back of my skull. I was thrown across the wheel and winded hard; behind me there was a crash and a spangle of jarred, unpleasant sounds, and I knew something had fallen.

The yawl had spun off course but I didn't bother to correct the wheel, instead heaving myself off the spokes and turning my head. The sail fluttered and in a wedge of space between the fabric and the boom I saw it:

The barrel.

"No!" I said, keening forward and ducking under the sail. Scrambling across the deck, I lurched for the toppled barrel; it had fallen onto its side and rolled, now, toward the railings; a spray of ice had exploded from the top and scattered across the deck; my catch lay sprawled on its front.

Its flesh was a pale and sickly yellow, the colour of spoilt milk. Its legs were tangled together, still half-inside the barrel; its bones seemed too angular, too sharp, pushing and poking against the inside of its skin to create nubs and points of pure white. It had been bald when I had pulled it from the water; now, impossibly, the rheumy dome of its skull was wispy with sodden tufts of black. Thankfully its head was turned away. One arm was pressed beneath its malnourished stomach and its hand was splayed under its jaw, the pale fingers like wormy tendrils spilling from its mouth.

The deck had stopped bucking and I moved cautiously toward the overturned barrel, eyeing my father's whaling harpoon as I approached. Gingerly I gripped the lip of the keg and lifted, my eyes never leaving the back of the creature's head. Its legs flopped out as I turned the barrel upright. Still it didn't seem to be breathing.

Throw it back.

Heart pounding, I crouched beside the creature and slipped my hands around its midsection. The thing was ice-cold and slick, but thankfully I felt no pulse through its knotted ribs. Grunting, I heaved it onto its knees and prepared to fold it back into the barrel.

Its head rolled back, eyes flashing as they caught the sun, and once again I was confronted with that face, that dreadful face…

Glancing toward the dogger bank to ensure I was not close enough to be watched, I steeled myself and slopped the creature back into the barrel. I knew that the simplest course of action would be to take the thing by the arms and drop it into the ocean, but I couldn't. Not without knowing the truth.

I gathered what ice I could and filled the keg to the creature's neck. I would need more. It screamed silently up at me, its face seeming to have more colour now. Its cheeks were no longer the sallow blue they had been, but a sickly pink.

Throw it back. Throw it anywhere. Throw it now.

The inside of its mouth was a pure, night black. The colour of the deepest sea.

6

Fog beat at the rocks behind me and billowed out from the edges of the clearing, generated as a fine mist by the still water beneath me and becoming a putrid yellow cloud by the time it reached the stone belt.

I gazed down into the water, horrified.

There must have been three or four dozen of them, floating on the surface. They lay on their fronts, their arms and legs dangling in the water, their bald heads submerged so that it was evident they had long ago drowned. Three or four dozen bodies, the skin so pale it was near transparent, the veins beneath a dull, spidery grey. They appeared distinctly human – almost *perfectly* human, in an uncanny way – though there was no way to discern their gender; in fact each body looked nearly identical. They hung moveless on the surface as though suspended in air, the water clear enough for me to see their long, slender limbs drooping from them like knots of yellow seaweed. I could not see their faces.

I was surrounded. I began to count, as I imagine is only human; not three or four dozen but five at least – I lost count at sixty-six. They bobbed softly as a breeze rippled across the surface of the water. Bony spines poked at their fleshy backs, shoulder-blades like knives.

Every impulse firing in my brain told me to haul out of there, to dive back into the fog and rocks and get out of that strange, unearthly clearing now – even if it meant dashing the yawl to pieces – but of course I stayed. Fixated on the body nearest the boat, feeling sick to my stomach but uncontrollably curious. So I did what any idiot would do.

I drew a deep breath, inhaling brine and salt and something like bad eggs. I fetched my heaviest net and a fishing pole, threw off my oilskin and rolled up my sleeves, and with a sick twist in my chest I prepared to heave the nearest corpse aboard.

7

I woke to a crashing sound on the deck.

I staggered up from below, my head thumping, legs weak and tender. I had drunk myself to sleep and suffered through a barrage of nightmares – endless, swirling images of that clearing, the rocks, the pale bald bodies hanging in the water – and my throat was on fire, my stomach pressurised and denuded of warmth. When I came onto the deck I was smashed in the face by a wall of icy wind, the yawl keening back on a tall, purling wave; it dropped from the crest and I buckled, scrambling for a grip on the slippery deck.

Hair batted my face as I turned my head toward the barrel and saw it rolling empty toward the railings. I screamed into the wind, watching powerlessly as it tipped through and fell into the water below. I clambered desperately to my feet, ducking under the swinging boom and rushing for the whaling harpoon. Perhaps the thing had fallen into the ocean with the barrel, I thought, perhaps—

I wheeled around at the sound of a wet, slapping footstep behind me.

The *Hexenspinne* smacked another wave and I raised the harpoon as the creature stepped forward, a wall of spray separating us. Through the mist I saw its face – my face – and balked, tightening my fingers around the shaft of the weapon. The barbed mouth of the harpoon glinted in the moonlight. "You're dead!" I yelled. "You were dead, god damn you!"

The creature stared back at me, its eyes blank and vacuous, its lips slightly open in a wet, dark smile. The tufts of hair sprouting from its bald, yellowish skull were thicker, more colourful now. Almost brown. Muscles and cable-like veins had begun to form on its arms and neck, shaping the otherwise limp and featureless form of its body.

It looked more like me now than it had done the night I'd pulled it aboard.

It took another step forward, standing with its arms hanging by its sides, its shoulders crooked to the left. Its chest rose and fell as though breathing were an effort; I supposed it must be. When I had found them in the water, they had been submerged... perhaps it wasn't accustomed to taking in air like this. It didn't seem to have any gills – but had they disappeared as it grew more recognisably human? I'd never been able to take a good look that night – and once I'd seen its face, I hadn't wanted to...

"Get back," I said, thrusting the harpoon forward like a spear as I stumbled back into the mast. "Get away, devil."

Ocean-water drooled down the creature's chin as its smile grew wider.

Its flesh was taut and pale, though colour had blossomed across its chest and genitals. I recognised a scar on its left shoulder, where a fishhook had ripped out a hunk of skin as a child: *my* scar, *my* shoulder. Its eyes were the same bright blue as mine, though they appeared remarkably more focused than I imagine mine had ever been. Every detail of its face matched my own, save for the colour – and even that, it was gaining.

"What are you?" I whispered.

My pale double lurched forward again, reaching with pale fingers. The smooth tips of those digits had begun to sharpen, fingernails growing from nubs of bone. I tightened my grip and aimed the harpoon at the creature's face. My god, it had even replicated the mole on my neck, beneath the left ear: it was a dull grey now, pressing against the thing's creamy flesh from the inside, but soon it would turn brown and dark.

Soon, the thing would be indiscernible from me.

I had thought, perhaps, that I had stumbled onto some dumping-ground for the rejects of a twisted experiment. That maybe the East India Trading Company had been toying with artificial doppelgangers, discarding the dead and rejected into the clearing... that I had dragged my own double aboard purely by chance.

Now, noting the hunger in the creature's expression, I was confronted with a terrible realisation: they hadn't been lying dead in the water, they hadn't been discarded...

They had been sleeping.

They just *slept* like that.

And I had offered myself; I had allowed it to steal my likeness. It hadn't had my face

"To what end?" I murmured, ocean spray beating my face, my teeth gritted against the wind. The yawl rocked and swung and I wondered how many faces had been stolen this way. How many fishermen had I met at harbour? How many of them had come from the very same clearing I had sailed into, or one like it? Swiping my harpoon blindly at the creature, I screamed: "*What do you want from me?!*"

Water ran from its eyes and nose in thin, clear runnels. My eyes, my nose. It flexed its fingers – my fingers, still tinged with yellow but distinctly mine –

and opened its mouth and laughed.

My laugh.

But not quite. The laughter was thick and low and gurgling, surging with a rattle that became a wheeze and stretched into a long, low bellow, a sound from the very depths of the sea. Then it lunged at me through the spray and clamped its hands around my throat.

8

The tiny yawl had lain askew at the edge of the dogger bank for more than a day. The sail was up, and fluttered in the wind, but the hull of the little boat was buried in a small crescent of grey sand, poking out of the calm water.

"Hello?" Harris called, slowing his tender as he approached the *Hexenspinne*. The weather was beginning to turn; he had anchored his own fishing vessel a little way from the sandbank in case of a sudden spell of harsh wind. He piloted his dinghy cautiously to the stern of the yawl and stood, unfurling a length of sodden rope. "Hello, there? Anybody aboard?"

When nobody replied he tossed up the rope and notched it onto the yawl's railings, then pulled slowly alongside the boat. As the tender gently thumped the yawl's hull, he glanced back to his own vessel and drew a breath. The horizon was turgid with creamy fog, stormclouds above bristling with energy. Trepid, he took the rope in both hands and heaved himself aboard the *Hexenspinne*.

"Hello, there?" he called again as he climbed over the railings. "I say, hell—"

He froze as he saw the man lying on the deck.

"Oh, Christ," Harris whispered, hurrying to the man's side and buckling into an awkward half-crouch beside him. He dug into the neck of the man's coat and pressed the pads of his fingers to his neck, cringing at the coolness of the skin. There was no pulse, he noted with dismay. His fingers came away red and wet. A blossom of crimson had spread across the poor sod's shirts, staining the fabric; his face was bruised, eyes rolled up in his head. God, what had happened here? Harris moaned as the smell of blood invaded his throat, scrambling to his feet. He ran both hands through his hair, a sick knot tightening his stomach.

His eyes lowered to a bloody harpoon, rolling softly across the deck. "Oh…"

Harris heaved, stumbling to the rails and vomiting overboard. Head spinning, he turned back and looked up at the mast. The sail was spattered with blood.

"*Help…*" came a rattling voice from behind the wheel. Good god, he hadn't even noticed the second body. Harris lurched forward, the yawl swaying beneath him. He grabbed the wheel to steady himself, stumbling toward the figure propped against the pedestal.

His heart stopped in his chest as he saw the second man's face.

The man was pale, blood stemming from a wound in his chest. His hand trembled as he reached up to take Harris' arm. "*Help me...*"

Twins, Harris thought. "What the hell had happened here?" he choked.

"He... attacked me..." the man wheezed.

The hunched thing at Harris' feet tightened its grip on his arm, coughing wetly.

A scuffle, then. A brotherly disagreement, perhaps. It didn't matter. Clearly the man had acted in self-defence: his neck had been slashed, his lower jaw slack and sloppy with blood; his stomach was painted red and his left leg was still softly pumping fluid into the water on the deck.

"Come on," Harris said, extending a hand to pull up the poor creature. He glanced at the corpse lying in the shadow of the fluttering sail, then back to the sputtering thing slumped against the wheel. "Let's get you to shore."

"Thank you," the man rattled, taking Harris' hand and stumbling to his feet. He smiled thinly and a trickle of water ran out of his mouth. He wiped it away. "I feel like I've been waiting my whole life to hear those words."

Author's Note:

This story, and a few others (none of which have been released as of today, and very few of which ever will be) exist within the world of a horror novel I am writing, on-and-off, called The Horror at Mustard Point. *While "Ice Blue" (originally called "Dead in the Water" – original, I know) was only meant to be an exercise in scene-setting to get me in the mood to write a huge* Mustard Point *scene, it quickly evolved into something much more. It might be a little too obvious for everyone else, but sometimes the best endings are the ones that you can see coming if you just squint a little into the mist.*

GREEN

The forest bristled with life as she tumbled through it, half-running, half-staggering with the bundle of burlap gripped tightly against her chest. It had stopped wriggling. Roots and ragged, wormy branches clawed at her feet and tangles of thicket grabbed her ankles and threatened to throw her into the crawling undergrowth.

Ducking under a hanging oak branch—a limb severed from its owner by what could only have been a bolt of lightning and dangling only from a knot of black, twisted wood—she chanced a look back into the dappled amber of the forest behind her. Nothing. Perhaps he'd given up. She clutched the still-warm bundle to her breast and scanned the trees, looking beyond them to the wheat-fields that crackled and bent in the wind. Peering between tall, thick pines and into the dark. He was gone. He was gone. She was—

Crack!

The blast of the shotgun echoed, made her head pound. Ears ringing. The oak tree beside her exploded: chunks of rich, brown bark showered the earth at her feet. Shocked, she stumbled back, her ankle catching on a thick, gnarled root of that same gargantuan tree.

Tripped.

The bundle fell from her arms and into the dirt as she stumbled to right herself. The two pheasants she'd wrung from her traps slid out of the burlap bag and gawped silently at her from the muck, their throats tight, eyes wide and terrified. She bent down, reaching desperately for them, for the only thing that would keep her and the children fed over the next couple of days. For her livelihood.

She froze. Saw him in the shadows, barely thirty yards away. He was not the same man she'd seen out in the wheat-field, the big, pot-bellied man in the lumberjack shirt that she'd run from in the first place. This pale, shuddering figure was younger, scrawnier, brandishing a sawn-off shotgun in one arm and a long-handled axe in the other. He grinned at her, mouth ripping open to flash rows and rows of tombstone teeth. He was naked, his flesh soft and pink and clinging to his bones. Slowly, with a single arm, he raised the shotgun and pointed it across her face. Her eyes widened.

Crack!

She was already running when she realised that a sliver of shrapnel from the shotgun blast had sliced through her calf. Warmth spread across her leg and trickled down her heel. Deep, gluey red drops beaded from the welt and scattered the forest floor behind her as she hurtled forward, the pheasants abandoned, forgotten.

She ran with the wheat-fields on her left, separated from the woods by a three-foot fence of barbed wire. She had thought the *We Will Prosecute* sign meant that they would get the police involved, but—god—they were trying to kill her. They were actually trying to kill her. She glanced out into the fields now and saw a dark smudge walking parallel with her, a dark smudge in a lumberjack shirt. Powerful strides carried the huge figure forward with a surprising grace; he kept up with her easily. His hands were empty, but she was more frightened of the heavyset man than she was of the scrawny bastard with the gun.

She had seen what he'd done to the last poacher caught out here.

She turned, hobbling away from the fence, aware that the farther she ran, the deeper into private land she came. There was no turning back now, not with what she assumed was the huge man's son in the woods with her. The only way was forward. Find somewhere to hide, to wait, then don't make a *fucking* sound—

Downhill. She was running downhill, and the trees were thinning, separating from each other, thick bunches of daylight shunting them apart. She could hear frogs croaking, dozens of them, their combined chirping a rumble of lurid madness. The green cracked open and she saw fire, the blazing hot gold of the sunset as ribbons of pink were sucked into the horizon and split open, erupting into shards of purple and ripped-up red.

Colours surrounded her as she fell out of the woods and into a meadow. Tall, wild grass danced madly around her as the sickly breeze that had trickled weakly through the forest turned to a stream of crashing, powerful wind and almost knocked her over. She was caught in a funnel of it; ahead, she saw a mess of thatch that looked like a wide expanse of rotten, wet reeds and, over to the right, across an unkempt expanse of wildflowers and grasses, the house. An old, crumbling farmhouse that had once been painted red but that had been bleached and drained by the sunlight and the years and was now an awful, fleshy pink.

She turned to look over her shoulder. No movement in the trees behind her that climbed and bent up the hillock. No sign of the giant in the lumberjack shirt or the naked imp that she presumed was his son. Now was her chance.

She bolted.

Blood spat from the wound in her calf as she headed for the thatch. She could hide there awhile, wait for dark, wait for them to call it a night and then run back through the woods. They wouldn't actually kill her. They couldn't. If anything, those shotgun blasts had been a warning, and his grazing her calf an accident.

But he was naked. And the look in his eyes, that horrible grin...

He was fucking insane. They both were.

The chirruping of frogs grew louder as she neared the reeds, a screaming, crackling electricity that thrummed through the ground. She saw slices of blue-grey between knots of thatch and figured the reeds must surround a pond of some considerable size; as she staggered closer, she caught an upwind whiff of the sour, hot smell of the water. Carbon dioxide and hydrogen sulphide breaking up beneath the surface; bad meat and eggs above.

She staggered into the reeds and paused, catching her breath. Turned, looked back. The two men were gone, and the forest was a blotted mass of darkness on the hillside. She stepped back, stepped back—

Her hip bumped something solid and sharp. She jolted, wheeled around—reeds scratching at her neck and back—and looked up.

A digger, parked leerily in the reeds—no, not parked, but abandoned, left here—with its bucket hanging into the water. Thick, black muck spilled out over the scoop's metal teeth. Rust sprayed the yellow walls of the cab and she could see inside through greasy, smeared windows. The machine was huge and she wondered how sunk into the boggy earth it must be for her to have missed it before. She grunted, reaching up, grabbing for the doorhandle. She couldn't hide in here, that was too obvious—if they figured she'd come to the pond, then this would be the first place they'd look—but perhaps there was something inside she could use to defend herself.

"Come out, come out, little chicken!" came a reedy voice from the meadow. It carried oddly on the wind, at once both strangled and screaming.

She swallowed as the door swung open and climbed inside the cab.

The seat was sunken and the wheel snapped off, leaving a sharp cylindrical mound jutting from a years-old dashboard. The levers were rusted in place. She moved awkwardly between the seat and the footbed, looking for something she could snap off, something she could break.

"Oh, chiii-iiicken!" called another voice. Female.

She kicked at one of the levers, hoping it would come loose. It bent in the middle but didn't break off. She winced, kicking out again—

Something moved in the reeds, just outside the cab window. A flash of shadow. The smell of damp earth. She clamped a hand over her mouth, froze in place. Refused to breathe, to move, to *look*. It was the imp from the woods, the wretch with the shotgun and the axe. She knew it.

"Come out, chicken…" he whispered, and his voice was behind her.

Slowly, she turned her head. The glass above her

was pink with smeared blood, grains of dirt sprayed across it. Thatch batted at the window outside. Nothing there. Nobody. She turned back—

And the door swung shut.

She screamed as the giant in the lumberjack shirt pressed his face against the glass. His eyes were dead, not just cold and emotionless but long sapped of any life at all, grey and hollow and rheumy. He was massive, and bending down just to look in at her through the window. Slowly, he smiled, a thin crack splitting his stubbled, loose-skinned face wide open. Oh god, it really was. His mouth was stitched shut. Thin, black ribbon curling through his lips, pressing them together. As his tongue pushed through, miniscule rivers of blood drizzled from the stitches.

Groan of metal. Her head snapped up and she saw the imp, through a hole in the ceiling, crawling over the cab above her. Screamed again as his wet, bony hand slapped the thick, curved windscreen, leaving a filthy print in the dust. The croaking of the frogs was louder, all around her, a lustful roar. Her eyes squeezed shut, she drew in deep, ragged breaths.

"What do you want from me?!" she yelled. "Christ, what do you want?!"

The imp knocked on the front of the digger. *Chunk. Chunk. Chunk.* A signal.

"*What do you want?!*" she screamed.

Silence.

"Please..." she whimpered. "Please, please don't..."

Nothing.

Slowly, she opened her eyes.

The giant at the window had gone, but there were bloody imprints where he had pressed his gurning face to the glass. She looked up; the naked imp had dragged himself back into the reeds.

She was alone.

"Oh, Christ," she whispered, laying a hand over her chest. Her heartbeat pounded and fluttered and her ribs smacked her palm. *Chunkchunkchunk.*

She heard a single croak, somewhere beneath the beached digger.

"What—"

Then it tipped forward. A shriek of rusted metal on metal as the whole thing pitched toward the water's surface, the bucket plunging into the pond as the ground beneath caved in and under. She moaned in agony as she was slammed into the dash, clawed at the steering arch where the wheel had been, dragged herself up—

The windscreen was covered. Frogs crawled up from the pond, dozens—hundreds, *thousands*—of them, smacking their webbed feet against the glass and batting their throbbing, yellow throats as they chirped and groaned. The weight of them on the front of the digger—Christ, streaming over it, stomping over each other, jumping from the bucket to the crane arm and then onto the glass with a thick, wet *smack*—was pulling it forward, dragging it into the mire, and all the while her window shrunk, fat bodies writhing over each other and filling in the sunlight.

And in the last moment before everything went black, she saw him. Standing waist-high in the water, sludge dripping off him in streams of grey and brown. His whole body was covered in a sluice of mucus-like pondwater, his skin a pale, deathly green. His smile was sickening, his head tipped to one side. He wore rags. They leapt around him, his amphibious minions, tiny bodies swarming the water at his waist. Swimming toward her.

Then the digger tipped and the blackened window went *smack* and there was water everywhere and she couldn't see a damn thing but she could feel the cold, the wet smashing inside, feel *them* everywhere, slimy bellies dragging across her face, slapping, webbed feet pressing at the muscles beneath all over her body.

Then the croaking was a thunderstorm, and the rain—everywhere, all at once—was enough to drown her.

Through bleary eyes, she saw shapes. Dark, flitting shapes in the red shadows of a firelit cavern, a cell of rough concrete and salt-encrusted bars, streaks of blood and gold running down the walls. She smelled pondwater again and felt the heat from it rising to her face, thought for a moment that she was still in that frigid water, still flailing—but then she tipped her head back and pain ripped through her skull and she realised she was sat on a stiff wooden stool, her ankles and wrists screaming with pain; cable ties, pulled tight so that her flesh was pinned to the sore bones beneath.

"Where…" she moaned, but she knew where. She didn't know how, or why… but she knew where they'd dragged her. Her eyes dropped and she found the source of the damp smell beneath her: a bowl of something grey and pulpy on the dirt floor, steam wafting up into her face. Dinnertime, she thought, and almost broke into hysterics.

"It's awake," someone whispered. Child's voice. Whiny. "Can we start now?"

"Wait, Peach. Patience." A woman. Husky, almost a breath. "She must eat first."

She looked up and saw them. The grey-haired behemoth in the checked shirt stood behind the bars, and she noticed that his lips had been stitched together again. In a shadowy corner of the room, the ghoulish figure from the woods stood scratching his crotch, shoulder jerking violently. He wore a pair of tattered dungarees, slung loosely across his otherwise-bare flesh. His clawing hand was stuffed into them.

Both of them were watching her hungrily.

And before her, a woman—was this the same one she'd heard out in the meadow?—sat on the floor with her hands folded, long, elegant fingers knotted together in prayer. Her eyes were closed. Her hair was cut close to the scalp and patchy, but she was strangely beautiful. A bruise-coloured dress clung to her body and where her arms and slim throat were exposed they were bone-pale.

"You have questions," she said, eyes snapping open and flickering toward the bound woman.

She nodded. Her head slopped about on her shoulders; had they drugged her? Christ, was she dying? Pain throbbed from her skull to her feet and back up again and she couldn't tell which parts hurt the most. She could smell burned metal. Tried to look into a square of bleeding light at one side that she thought might be a doorway, but only saw a mess of roots thrusting through a broken window, filling it, lit by a crooked lantern so that gold sprayed them like paint. The cell was in ruins. Fungus rippled across the edges of the ceiling, ribbons of yellow and gold.

Deep in the house, something croaked.

"Where am I?" she rasped.

"You're in our home."

"The things in the pond—"

"—the frogs—"

"—and that *man*..."

The woman smiled. "You are delirious. You were

imagining him."

"You're lying."

"Yes."

Silence. Her heart screamed against the bars of its cage and her head pounded, blood thumping in her ears.

"I have kids," she said. "Please, they'll know something's happened, they'll know I came here—"

"And if they come looking for you, we shall let him have them."

Her blood ran cold. Stopped pounding. Stopped pumping. "No."

"Pray they have more sense than their kin."

She swallowed. Thought about the figure in the pond. "Who was he?"

The woman sighed. "We—down, Peach—we call him the Master in the Water."

She looked, her head swinging like a weight on a string. Peach—the foul thing from the woods—was halfway up the wall, scuttling like an insect, his arms bent out, claws dug into the concrete. Drool hung from his mouth in thick, gluey strings.

"Who are *you*?"

The woman smiled thinly. "You can call me Mother. You've met Peach—and my husband, Malachi. Do forgive his rambling."

She cocked an eyebrow. Her head was sore.

"And this is my daughter, Messalina."

She noticed movement in the corner of her eye—over her shoulder, behind—and craned her neck to look. A girl sat on a stained mattress, ragged hair falling about a gaunt, pale face. She could only have been ten or eleven. It was difficult to say, because the girl's hands were in her eyes.

The bound woman frowned. No, the girl's hands were really *in* her eyes. Her fingers were gouged into two empty sockets, and thin trails of red gore ran across her palms.

"Is she a witch?" the bound woman asked.

"She would have been," Mother nodded, "many years ago. But no—she simply sees."

"How?"

Mother smiled as the woman in the chair turned back to face her. "He allows it."

"He?"

"Master."

The woman swallowed. "In the pond. I thought... I thought you'd left me to die there. with him." She remembered the frogs, crawling over the abandoned digger, over each other. "With them."

"Oh, we had," Mother blinked, as if stung by the obviousness of the woman's statement. "But he has other plans for you. You're not like the others."

"Others?"

"Food," Peach giggled. The woman looked up. He was on the ceiling, eyes wild and huge in his sunken face.

"What does he want with me?"

Mother sighed. "His body grows tired of him. He needs another."

"You're insane," she spat.

"Possibly. Anyway… rest a while. Eat. Look—breakfast."

Mother reached forward, nudging the bowl closer with a horrible scraping sound.

"Eggs," she whispered.

The woman in the chair looked down. Grey goop swilled about in the shallow bowl. There was texture to it—it was lumpy. No, the sludge was *lumps*. It was made up of hundreds of tiny, spherical sacs of translucent, mucus-like balls, all gathered in one gluey membrane…

Frogspawn, she realised, seeing tiny black dots inside each boiled, wet sphere. "Oh, Jesus…"

She kicked out. Her ankles were tied together; both feet smashed into the bowl and sent it spinning, tipping out onto the floor. Above her, Peach howled.

Mother's face changed. "That was a gift," she said quietly. "Master is usually so… precious, with his eggs. How *dare* you?"

Behind the bars, the giant—Malachi—moaned through his stitched-up lips. On the ceiling, Peach giggled like a child.

"All right, that's enough," Mother said, standing

suddenly, brushing the dust and shadows from her dress. She clapped her hands, once. "Peach, take your father outside."

"Mother—"

"Now!" Mother snapped, her eyes never leaving the bruised woman in the chair. "Out! Both of you!"

Skittering as Peach crawled toward the bars. Screaming sound of metal on metal. Shadows looming as the bars fell away and then swung in again.

Mother smiled down at her. "A little rest and some food would have made this all so much less painful for you," she said. "But since you're not hungry…"

"Let me go," the poacher said, "please, you don't need to do this, let me—"

"Mess, take her to the cellar."

Hands clapped over her eyes—a little girl's hands, stained with blood—and she screamed as a thick, inky darkness flooded into her and everything went black.

Air sucked into lungs. Stink of rotten tomatoes. Throbbing. Croaking.

Gasping awake.

"Shit!" she yelled, breathing fast, chest ragged. Trying to move, to stand—too weak. She flopped back down. Laid on the ground. Dusty floor. Sand?

Damp. Everywhere. And a shape… his shape. The Master in the Water. Standing over her.

More croaks. All around. A voice: "Feed her."

Girl in her vision. Little girl. No eyes. Bloody holes in face. Hands red and screaming. Pouring, tipping something into her mouth.

Warm, wet slop. Lumpy. Sacs of mucus popping between teeth. Gagging. Vomiting – pushed back down, forced back down by more of the putrid, spoiled stuff.

Black. Corners of eyes going dark. Protesting – exhaustion. Pain.

Sleep.

When she awoke again, she was curled up in the foetal position, laying on her right side in the dirt. Hands clasped beneath a cheek sticky with drool, one foot laid across the other. Her ribs and back ached, her mouth dry and acrid. She could smell sulphur and incense.

She blinked herself alert, looking around, easing herself up. Groggy, disoriented.

She sat in a circle of white powder, sprinkled into the dirt. Three rough, concentric rings ripped into the shadows that spilled across the floor. The ground beneath her was bumpy, not flat but rippling like a shallow dune; looking out toward the cellar walls, she saw that the floor at the edges of the chamber dipped and fell away, swallowed by pools of thick, grey water. She was on a little island in the middle of it all, a moat of pond scum. Blossoms of frogspawn sprouted from the water, climbing the walls—knots and bundles of it running in upward trails like heavy, slick ivy plants.

There were frogs all around, their chirping a steady, low hum. They sat in the water, beady, black eyes glistening, tiny points of amber light reflected in them and turning them demonic and benevolent. Some encroached the edge of her little island of silty sand, but none came within the first circle. She was dry; something had carried her here.

"He's coming now," came a soft, female voice from the corner of the cellar.

She craned her neck, wincing at the agony that pulsed through the tendons in her tight, bunched shoulder muscles. Saw the little girl from before sat on a low writing desk, its legs half-submerged in the water at the edge of the room. Messalina. A wire shelf beneath the desk sagged in the middle; pinpricks of light dashed the darkness of the little alcove in pairs. Eyes looking out. More frogs sat on the table itself, and one—a fat, spiny brown thing—rested in Messalina's cupped hands, its bloated, yellow girth bulging between her fingers.

She was looking at the woman in the white circle, looking without eyes. "I see what he sees," said the girl. "I see the kitchen. He moves slowly. He'll be here soon, though. The way to the cellar is through the door beneath the stairs. He's in the hallway now."

"Please," she begged. Her voice was hoarse. She wondered how long she'd been out. Hours? Days? "Please, don't—"

"Crawlspace," the girl whispered.

The woman frowned. "I don't under—"

"Shh," Messalina said. "He's he-ere…"

The woman turned. Her eyes moved over crooked shelves bracketed to the walls, crude ironwork framing them. Candles blazed, jammed into the sockets of little, polished skulls. Wax dribbled over grinning jaws and dripped over the edges of the shelves into the softly-lapping water beneath. Arcane symbols were scratched into the concrete, half-obscured by strings of twitching, bubbling frogspawn. The croaking was unbearable, and the rubbery creatures were everywhere. Crawling over each other, bobbing in the water, climbing with long, stretched back limbs over abandoned chairs and tables, legs broken and sharp. Wide mouths in blank, black-eyed faces. Pulsing bellies stricken through with pale, green veins.

A door screamed open.

She turned her head toward the sound—and saw it. A square, crude hole in the wall, water swilling at its mouth. Barely at knee height, if that at all. Darkness beyond; where did it go? Was this the crawlspace? Was the girl trying to *help* her?

Her eyes flitted up to the door, and she saw him.

Master was tall and slender, his hands hanging past

his knees. His clothes were the remnants of black robes, eaten and worn by many inclement years—decades? *centuries?*—so that they clung to his narrow figure in rags. His legs were exposed, and the skin was the same sickly, pale green as the frogs' bellies. Run through with the same veins, patchy and mottled yellow inside his thighs. His arms were the same, though they were covered with brown, blotchy horns and stubs like the back of the toad in Messalina's lap.

His face was a mask of death. His expression was blank—the vacant, uninterested look of a frog—but it was pallid and tight against a bald, slick skull. His entire body was coated in mucus and flecks of seaweed.

He said, "I won't hurt you," and she almost believed him. His voice was a dry croak, as if he hadn't spoken in years. When he stepped into the room, his feet—toes webbed, veins bulging against the skin—splashed softly in the water. His fingers twitched at his knees. He said, "Do you believe in God?" and for a moment she did.

"That isn't what you are," she whispered.

He smiled, his mouth spreading wider rather than turning upward. His throat bulged with every breath. At his feet, the frogs and toads grew excited, their own bodies pulsing with a sickening, almost lustful kind of admiration for the man in the sodden clothes. "I am a god to them," he said. She didn't know if he meant the frogs or the family. She wondered where Mother had gone. Had she simply left Messalina to take care of this? "I have given them such gifts," Master continued, speaking slowly, softly. Carefully, as though each word were an effort. "Longer lives. More illustrious lives. Kept them fed, kept their bellies, their crops… moist. I live peacefully in the pond, and I eat when I am given food."

"This is sick," she said, "this is all *sick*—"

"Let Master speak," Messalina hissed behind her.

Master's smile fell. "Ah, the prophet," he whispered. "I have grown fond of the child."

"What did you do to her?"

"Allowed her to see. To see through my eyes, and yours… to bestow both sight and darkness upon others. A touch of the child's hands, and you might see all the secrets of the universe… or be blinded forever."

"And what about the others? What do they get for… for worshipping you?"

"They get to live," Master said, and he stepped forward. The door swung shut behind him as the water swallowed his ankles. He glided toward her, raising a hand. He waved it a little.

All at once, the candles flared around her and orange light erupted across the ceiling. She looked up, saw more symbols carved into the concrete: three concentric rings, mirroring the ones beneath her so that she felt she was trapped in some invisible pillar or his knees. His clothes were the remnants of black robes, eaten and worn by many inclement years—decades? *centuries?*—so that they clung to his narrow figure in rags. His legs were exposed, and the skin was the same sickly, pale green as the frogs' bellies. Run through with the same veins, patchy and mottled yellow inside his thighs. His arms were the same, though they were covered with brown, blotchy horns and stubs like the back of the toad in Messalina's lap.

His face was a mask of death. His expression was blank—the vacant, uninterested look of a frog—but it was pallid and tight against a bald, slick skull. His entire body was coated in mucus and flecks of seaweed.

He said, "I won't hurt you," and she almost believed him. His voice was a dry croak, as if he hadn't spoken in years. When he stepped into the room, his feet—toes webbed, veins bulging against the skin—splashed softly in the water. His fingers twitched at his knees. He said, "Do you believe in God?" and for a moment she did.

"That isn't what you are," she whispered.

He smiled, his mouth spreading wider rather than turning upward. His throat bulged with every breath. At his feet, the frogs and toads grew excited, their own bodies pulsing with a sickening, almost lustful kind of admiration for the man in the sodden clothes. "I am a god to them," he said. She didn't know if he meant the frogs or the family. She wondered where Mother had gone. Had she simply left Messalina to take care of this? "I have given them such gifts," Master continued, speaking slowly, softly. Carefully, as though each word were an effort. "Longer lives. More illustrious lives. Kept them fed, kept their bellies, their crops… moist. I live peacefully in the pond, and I eat when I am given food."

"This is sick," she said, "this is all *sick*—"

"Let Master speak," Messalina hissed behind her.

Master's smile fell. "Ah, the prophet," he whispered. "I have grown fond of the child."

"What did you do to her?"

"Allowed her to see. To see through my eyes, and yours… to bestow both sight and darkness upon others. A touch of the child's hands, and you might see all the secrets of the universe… or be blinded forever."

"And what about the others? What do they get for… for worshipping you?"

"They get to live," Master said, and he stepped forward. The door swung shut behind him as the water swallowed his ankles. He glided toward her, raising a hand. He waved it a little.

All at once, the candles flared around her and orange light erupted across the ceiling. She looked up, saw more symbols carved into the concrete: three concentric rings, mirroring the ones beneath her so that she felt she was trapped in some invisible pillar or beam; symbols that looked like spliced letters and digits, like twisted figure-eights and scrawled, mad numbers. A spell, an incantation... a ritual.

The Master in the Water stood over her and showed her the back of his hand. She saw that the flesh was beginning to peel. "You understand," he whispered. "It will only be for a few years. And then your body will decay, too, and I will free you and inhabit another."

She whimpered. This wasn't happening, none of it. Christ, her kids...

A dull chant began to resound through the cellar. Not human voices... the frogs. There were no words, but their croaking had risen in volume, each so individually mangled and distorted that, together, they formed a single, low hum.

"Please..."

"You understand," said Master, and it was like he wanted her to, like he needed it. "Don't you?"

"Please!" she begged as the candlelight soared. She couldn't move, frozen to the spot by fear. Above her, sick, green shadows trickled through the indents and patterns in the ceiling. The water all around bubbled and boiled. Master bent forward—

And a pink shape leapt onto his back and clamped its hands over his eyes.

Her breath hitched in her throat as she saw black ink spread across the slender, green creature's face and then sink back into the sockets of his skull. He scrambled and clawed at the girl clinging to his back but she held tight, looking up at the woman in the white circle and yelling, screaming furiously: "Crawlspace! Now!"

She bolted, the agonised wail of the Master in the Water echoing about the drowned cellar like an air-raid siren as he sunk to his knees, clawing and scratching at his face. Water splashed her face as she plunged into the shallow pool at the wall's edge and scrambled for the crawlspace, ignoring the plops and whistles of the creatures all around her. Frogs and toads leapt onto her back and legs, sucking at her skin with their rubbery mouths as they clamped tiny, webbed feet to her flesh—

She wriggled through the hole, not daring to look back or to pause, diving headfirst into a tunnel barely wide enough for her shoulders to scrape through. Behind her, she heard the young girl shriek. Something hit a wall and went *thwump* and then she heard Master roaring, bellowing so loud that the tunnel shook.

She crawled forward, splashing madly through water that rose higher and higher, freezing her chest and then slicing at her neck. Full dark, nothing to guide her but the downward slope of the tunnel, and she could only hope that it wouldn't go down far enough that she ended up completely underwater—

There was a crash behind her and rubble showered her feet as Master plunged into the tunnel. "I can still *smell* you!" he screamed, and she looked back over her shoulder, saw pale green hands slam into the walls and claw at them, dragging him forward. His slender bulk blotted out the light from the candlelit cellar and she saw black rivers running like tar from his eyes, eyes which had exploded in his face and sprayed his discoloured flesh with ichor.

Kicking out at frogs that thrashed and bounced madly in the water around her, she crawled backward, straining her arms to keep her head above the surface, crying out as thick arms of pond-weed caught around her limbs and drew her back against the swell. More symbols in the walls, these lit by a light from… above?

She looked up. A hole, a tiny pinprick of light thirty feet above her. Rough, stone walls leading up. And rungs. A rusted, iron ladder embedded in the rock.

Freedom.

A hand wrapped around her ankle as she reached up to grab for the lowest rung. She screamed, kicking madly at the thick, heavy fingers, cold against her skin and so slippery and wet—the Master in the Water moaned as she smashed his knuckles into the tunnel wall and yanked her calf free, spitting water as she grabbed the rod and pulled. Hauling herself up—up, up to the top rung, exhaustion crackling like burning wood in her chest. She swore. The ladder stopped. Still a long way to climb. She couldn't. Looked down. Master climbing after her. No…

For your kids, she thought desperately. Do it for them. Keep going!

Digging her fingers into the stone, she clawed madly and hauled herself higher, scrambling for the light at the top of the tunnel, heaving her wracked body up the well. As she climbed it narrowed, the walls caving in so that her shoulder-blades were scraped raw by the stone behind her and she had to push with her feet to climb. She felt her fingernails chipping and splintering, felt warm welts begin at her fingertips, heard Master smashing his way up the well beneath her—

"You're coming with me," he whispered, his voice more like the strained chirrup of a frog than anything, and she felt his face brush her heel.

"Bollocks I am!" she yelled, and kicked down, hard.

Teeth clamped down on her ankle and she screamed, wet heat exploding from the ruptured flesh. She slipped, dropped—clinging to the wall with one hand while the other batted at the mad creature below, beating wildly at his face. Chunks tore from her heel—

And then he fell. In the half-light from above she saw his face contort in surprise, saw his rags flutter as he crumpled into the water beneath with a splash.

Then they were upon him, thousands of them, bloated, brown-green bodies swarming his flailing figure until all she could see of the bottom was a rippling mass of black.

"Come on!" she yelled, clawing her way up, adrenaline pushing her higher, faster, until her fingers dug for more flint and curled around the lip of the well. She heaved, wrenching her body out through the ragged opening and tearing strips from her skin on the sharp stone.

And then she was free.

She collapsed in the wild grass, laying for a moment with a brittle fog of sunlight falling and cascading over her. Free. The cool air brushed her face and she remembered daylight as though it had been years since she'd last felt it.

Relief flooded her body and she laughed, punching her fists into the ground and scrambling up onto her knees. She'd made it. Out of that awful house, that candlelit cesspit… away from the Master in the Water and the backwards family who…

No… the *family*…

Slowly, fearfully, she looked up.

Peach grinned down at her, his yellow teeth sprayed across blood-red gums. He had lost the dungarees and abandoned the shotgun, but he gripped the axe in both hands like he'd never held anything more precious.

"You're on private property, lady," he hissed, and then he shrieked with laughter and raised the axe high above his head.

Author's Note:

You have just read the first story I ever had published. "Green" first appeared in The Old Ways: Volume Two *(2023) from Eerie River Press, and while I was excited to see that the rights had reverted back to me so I could print it again, I will forever be grateful to everyone at Eerie River for taking that chance on me. The publication of this story in that otherwise-fantastic anthology (please do check it out – the authors within are highly deserving of your attention) arguably kicked off my horror career. Before I had even submitted this story anywhere, I had planned to release it myself in a collection of three, also including "Red" and "Amber". I'm glad to finally bring that dream to life now, in* Marsh Lights, *though – as you can probably tell – plans changed ever so slightly in the meantime.*

BLOOD RED

FLYTRAP (noun):
a carnivorous, flowering plant that, after snapping its jaws shut, secretes an enzyme to decompose its prey and consume the nutrients released.

Dana stood at the kitchen window with a mug of coffee and watched the snow fall.

The street outside was washed in the soft, grey light of the evening and the tarmac bled through in pools and scraps of shining, steely black; a thick crust of white lay across the road and shimmering ropes of dust wafted up and down in the wind. Out here on the outskirts of the city, traffic – even foot-traffic – was slow and sparse, and the snow had been allowed to pile up and chew at the edges of terraced houses, uninterrupted by gruelling tyres and footsteps. A single, battered Volvo was parked across from Dana's window. The windscreen was covered. A thin aerial poked out of a mound of white powder on the car's roof, twanging violently as the breeze pulled at it.

She took a long sip and smiled as a shadowy figure

waddled into view at the end of the street. Her slender fingers, locked around the mug, were stained with ink and correction fluid. Dark rings had soldered themselves beneath her eyes, and the lids were heavy with sleeplessness. For weeks, she had been hungry for something new. For inspiration.

Now, she watched him walk home.

Without looking behind her, she reached back for a stool and pulled it up to the kitchen sink. She sat, never taking her eyes off the figure in the snow. He was perfect.

For six years, Dana Collings had studied creative writing through the Open University. It might have been three or four, had she not been working two part-time jobs simultaneously (one at the Tea Barn down the road, and one at a little bar in Weeping), but in all honesty she had been grateful for the time. She had never been one of those head-in-the-game women who knew exactly what they wanted to do, who wanted everything, all of the time… she had wanted to write, and that was just about all she knew. So she had seen those six years as an opportunity to find out – to discover the kind of writing she liked, the kind she was good at, and to hope that they were one and the same.

And now, four years after her graduation, Dana Collings had sold three stories, the script for a television pilot that never made it to air, and about six thousand slices of carrot cake at the Tea Barn. Ten years, she thought, watching through the window. Snow beat softly at the glass. Ten years, and I still don't know what the *fuck* I want to do with my life.

But she thought movies might be the way to go. She had begun sending her first full-length screenplay to agents in the summer, and although so far the only response she had had was from a man who told her *Calamity* would only make it to the screen if she suddenly died and, posthumously, became a household name, she was hopeful.

At least, she had been hopeful. And then, in the last few weeks, when she had sat down to write her next film, she found that her wells had dried up. There was nothing. Sure, she had struggled with the ending for *Calamity* – but now, even the beginning of a new story was behind her.

"But here you are," she whispered, blinking slowly as the soft warmth of the coffee in her hands wafted up into her face. She kept her eyes on the boy – he could only have been seventeen or eighteen – as he walked along the street, sticking to the other side of the snow-ridden road. He was thin and gangly, even in a blue parka and ragged, red scarf; his legs were long and slender and his hands hung down by his thighs, blood-red gloves covered in flakes of white and grey. His face was narrow, his chin prickled with stubble. A thin band of acne crossed his neck like a rope burn.

Her fingers itched. She wanted to write. She *had* to

write. This was it. This boy, this snowbound figure, was her muse. Oh, she had seen plenty of people walk up and down this street in the last couple of weeks, but there was something different about this one. He had a story to tell. And she would tell it.

"I think I'll call you... Eric," she said quietly. Thin strands of dark, greying hair fell in Dana's face as she reached forward to set down her mug. Eric. That felt right. Felt like it really could be the kid's name. Truly, she felt a strange connection to him: there was nothing out-of-the-ordinary about the boy, but he compelled her. She felt like she knew him. Knew his history. Her eyes flickered to the rucksack on his shoulder. Dull, grey fabric and brown straps.

She wondered what was inside. Schoolbooks, maybe. No... she needed something more interesting than that. If she was going to make a film from this guy, she needed something... meaty.

Dana watched as the young man reached his door and stopped. His house was a narrow terrace, hemmed in by the others on either side. Drab, redbrick walls made pretty and damp by the snow. Narrow, blackened windows. Curtains drawn.

Maybe he was hiding something.

He stood at the doorway for a moment – the door was a pale shade of green – and fumbled in the pocket of his parka. Presumably, she thought, for his keys. He glanced over his shoulder, looked up and down the street.

Momentarily, they locked eyes. The briefest flash of a frown crossed his face, and then he turned back to the door.

His rucksack fell off his shoulder. He caught it, just before it hit the ground. Dana's gaze fell to the bag, and she saw that the bottom of the thing was damp. From being left in the snow?

No, something inside was leaking. Thin strings of moisture drooled through the fabric and connected it to the pavement.

Dana smiled. Almost sliding off her stool, she grabbed her mug and crossed the kitchen quickly, stepping through the hall into the living room. Her typewriter was positioned on the top of a cabinet by the wall, and she slid into an office chair and cracked her knuckles.

Picturing the boy's face, she closed her eyes and laid her hands on the keys.

What's in your bag? she thought. And there was her story. There was her film.

She began to write.

Outside, the young man had disappeared inside his home. The snow fell, hard, and in moments even his footsteps had vanished.

***

BUTCHER'S BOY
written by Dana Collings

INT. BLACKWOOD BUTCHER'S SHOP - DAY.

A quiet end to a slow day. The butcher's shop is closing up. **SFX:** the whirring of CHILLERS in the background as a meat cleaver CHOPS on a wooden board.

A big, muscular forearm swings into view and blood splatters the camera as the last cuts of the day are chopped and prepared. The butcher, **JOHN BLACKWOOD**, turns his head as a second, scrawnier figure appears in the background.

The scrawny figure, **ERIC** (late teens, brown hair, acne) swallows, stepping forward.

          ERIC
     You wanted to see me, boss?

Blackwood buries the cleaver in the wood with a CHOK. Slowly, he turns…

And he's all smiles. A burly, kind-looking, middle-aged man. Slightly sweaty and red-faced. Wearing a butcher's apron and a net over his beard.

BLACKWOOD
Take a pew.

He gestures to the back counter. Freshly cleaned. Eric looks at it reluctantly, and then hoists himself up, dropping a grey rucksack at his feet.

Blackwood leans back against the glass display shelves, full of meat. He smiles sadly.

BLACKWOOD
How long have you been stealing from us, Eric?

Eric falters. Terror in his eyes. His leg - the one nearest the rucksack - twitches.

   ERIC
 I… I haven't…

Blackwood raises a hand. *Stay calm.*

   BLACKWOOD
 It's okay. Hey, don't sweat. Listen, I know we can only pay you minimum wage. I know that… in this day and age… that might not be enough to get you by. I'm sorry.

   ERIC
 I haven't - I wouldn't…

   BLACKWOOD
 Listen to me, kid. I said, it's okay. People do silly

things when they're desperate. And I like you. You're not in any trouble. I just want you to be honest with me. I want you to keep working here – if you want to. Okay?

Eric hesitates. He's practically sweating some himself now.

ERIC
I didn't mean…

BLACKWOOD
I know. I know. And like I said, it's okay. Listen to me, whatever you've got in your little bag, there… Put it back. Put it on back, and we'll not mention this again. Give us a couple of months, kid, and we might even be able to give you a raise, okay?

Eric nods.

BLACKWOOD
Go on, now.

Slowly, Eric slides off the countertop. He lifts up the bag, unzips it. Reaches in and pulls out handfuls of meat. Eight sausages in a little carrier bag. Two packs of bacon. A side of lamb.

BLACKWOOD
That's it, you can leave it there. You know what? Take the sausages with you. But please… Eric, don't steal from me again. Okay? If you need help, at home, I can get you help –

ERIC
Thank you. For not firing me.

Blackwood nods.

        BLACKWOOD
If there's anything I can do –

        ERIC
   (shaking his head)
That's all right. I… it won't happen again, boss. I promise.

He zips up his bag and turns to leave. A close shot on his face reveals a single tear.
But he's not upset.

He's afraid.

Dana woke up the next morning to the sound of a slamming door.

Her eyes snapped open and she jerked upright, clawing at the sheets that had locked themselves around her throat and legs in the night. Cold slipped in through a narrow crack in the window-frame and ate hungrily at the room. Her eyes turned to the window. A little damp strip had gathered on the sill. Grunting, she heaved herself out of bed and, hair mussed up in a bird's nest around her face, the left leg of her pyjama bottoms rolled up to her knee, she moved to the window to pull the curtains closed.

She stopped when she saw him.

The master bedroom – the *only* bedroom, she reminded herself – of the little terraced house was positioned right above the kitchen, so that now, when she looked across the street, she could see the pale green door of the boy's home. Of her Eric's home. The Volvo had gone, and snow had almost filled in the square of grey tarmac left by its passing. The morning light was cold and pallid.

She watched as Eric tugged on his gloves and started walking away from the house, rucksack slung over his shoulder. He was limping.

Hadn't slept, she thought. All night, he must've been tossing and turning. He was exhausted. In pain…

Her eyes narrowed as he stopped walking. Quickly, he bent down and plucked at the bottom of his trouser leg. Rolled it up a little.

With shaking fingers, he fixed up a bandage wrapped around his ankle. No… all the way around his shin. Wound up half his leg like the gauze of a mummy. Dana could see blood seeping through the fabric and running in needle-thin rivers down into his shoe. Then Eric pulled down his trouser leg and kept walking.

Dana blinked.

He *was* in pain. For a moment, she mused over the strange connection she felt to him. She fancied she could almost have been dreaming about this, the images in her mind were so real. The rough edge of a breadknife – the long, slow drips of a leaky pipe in the boy's basement…

The screams…

"Oh, this is gold," she whispered. "This is *perfect*."

Eric limped away, awkwardly applying weight to his wounded leg, and Dana smiled.

INT. DANK CELLAR – NIGHT.

```
The butcher's boy cowers in a dark
corner, as close to the door as he
can be. Still in his work clothes,
but without the white apron. The
rucksack is somewhere upstairs.

Above, the house is silent. But here,
there are sounds: the DRIP of
something leaking.
```

The HEAVY BREATHING of the creature that's down here with him.

> **ERIC**
> Here… this is all I could get for you.

Slowly, he offers up a plate. Pinkish, translucent liquid swills over one edge. His hands are shaking.

On the plate are four sausages, still connected to each other at their ends in a fleshy string. The other four are in the kitchen upstairs. He still has to feed himself, after all.

Eric reaches into his back pocket and draws out a long, serrated breadknife. It GLINTS in the flickering light of a single bulb. Sweat runs down the boy's forehead. Despite the cold of the cellar, despite his shivering… there's a warmth down here. The body heat of the colossal CREATURE, just out of shot.

He looks up at it and nods.

>   **ERIC**
> Want some?

He lashes upwards with the breadknife, severing the connecting tissue between two sausages. Meaty juice splatters the shadows.

Laying the breadknife down on the plate, Eric picks up the loosened sausage and offers it, raw, in the palm of his hand.

There's a long, long pause. The lightbulb BUZZES noisily.

Then a thick, scratchy tongue lashes out of the darkness and THWAPS Eric's wrist. It's huge and long and wet and violently pink. Serrated edges bristle, like thin, papery teeth.

The sausage is knocked out of Eric's hand and rolls across the cellar. He cries out, stumbles back.

ERIC
Hey!

The long tongue reappears, swiping at the plate in his hand. Hungrily, it rolls around the other three sausages and envelops them, whipping back into the dark.

SFX: wet CHEWING.

The plate and knife fall and clatter to the ground. Eric stumbles to pick them up and backs away, towards the door. Jaw set, eyes wide.

As he fumbles for the handle, the tongue thrusts past him and SLAMS into the wood, holding the door closed.

ERIC
No… please. I tried to get more, but…

Long ropes of drool roll over his shoulder and he whimpers.

          ERIC
      (weakly)
     Please… I'll get more for you. Tomorrow. Please.

It's not good enough. The creature stirs. Although it's still out of shot, it fills all the space we can't see. It's huge. Hungry.

          ERIC
     Please.

His eyes falter. Fall onto the breadknife. Slowly, he drops to his knees and picks it up. Pauses.

He looks up again, eyes pleading, as if praying to God. The creature is not merciful.

Eric extends one leg, and rolls up

the leg of his trousers.

The tongue retreats. The sound of hungry lips smacking together ECHOES through the cellar.

Eric squeezes his eyes shut.

          ERIC
        (to himself)
    Oh, god…

And with a swift, brutal movement, he grinds the serrated blade of the knife into his shin, just above the ankle, and SCREAMS loudly as he peels the flesh all the way up to his knee. It falls away, a pale, pink rasher.

As the tongue laps it hungrily off the floor, Eric moves the blade to the back of his shin and continues to carve himself, SHRIEKING all the while.

            ***

The next few days passed quietly, and heavily. Dana's inspiration had shrunk away into that damp, squalid place at the back of her mind where most of her dreams had gone to die, and although she watched the young man's house from the kitchen window and, in the evenings, from her bedroom, she found nothing where that unnatural, almost intimate connection to him had been before. She felt like she had known him, briefly, seen him almost through the eyes of that creature in his basement, as if it was somehow more than just an imagined embellishment to his otherwise-plain decor. She had been able to picture the inside of the house as though she had been there with him; she had known his *name*.

And now, she thought, this was her prize for coming to know him – or, at least, the imagined version of him that was colourful enough to land the starring role in her film – so closely. Or perhaps it was her punishment for putting so much faith in her unknowing muse. Perhaps she was just suffering through another Dark Spot, and the inspiration would return, by itself, in time.

At the end of each shift at the Tea Barn, she returned home to take up her perch by the window. But she saw nothing. No movement for almost a week, except for one night when she saw – or thought she saw, perhaps – a little flicker of shadow in one window as the boy pulled his curtains across.

She didn't sleep.

She often struggled to, during her Dark Spots, and even gently upping her daily dose of citalopram failed to alleviate the spinning thoughts and heady, bloodthirsty spirals that kept her awake. On Thursday night, she stayed up at the typewriter until four in the morning, only to toss the eighteen pages she had written straight in the recycling when she finally woke up the next morning. On Saturday, after spending an hour at the kitchen window and seeing nothing interesting, she tried, again, to write. Her fingers hovered over the keys of the typewriter for what must have been hours. Nothing came to her. She tried to picture Eric's face and found that the image had almost entirely gone from her. She felt… hungry. Withering. And although she ate, when she remembered too, it didn't feel like enough. Everything was dark.

And she fell asleep at the typewriter.

She dreamed, after a while, of a cellar. She felt she had been here before. No, she had *written* about this place. The door was closed. She was alone. Alone, and hungry, and waiting…

And then the door opened.

Flickering light washed into the cellar, and Eric's silhouette stepped into the frame. With a bowed head, he came towards her, and said, "I'm sorry. I didn't mean to keep you waiting. I brought this –"

Her eyes snapped open.

Dana spluttered, reeling back in her chair. The typewriter rattled softly as her knee jerked up and the cabinet wobbled. She stood, coughing up dust. Blinking the sand out of her eyes, she glanced up at the clock on the living room wall and saw that she'd been asleep for most of the morning.

"Christ, what the…"

Her eyes fell onto the sheets of paper jamming up the crest of the typewriter. She looked down at her fingers. They were red, almost raw, from writing.

Perhaps she hadn't been asleep for as long as she thought.

"But I don't remember…" she whispered, stepping forwards. Three full pages. Three *good* pages. Oh, this stuff was it. This was the film she'd been trying to write.

And she couldn't remember writing it.

Still, she supposed, she was too tired to remember much of anything. But… no. She *did* remember. Remembered waking up with the first bands of a tension headache rippling behind her eyes. She had gone to the kitchen, gotten a mug of coffee. And she had seen…

What had she seen?

She had seen a light on downstairs. In the house across the street. That was all she had needed. Just a single, orange light. And she had come back to the typewriter and written, half-conscious, half-alive.

Dana remembered.

And so she settled back into her office chair and began to read.

INT. CELLAR - NIGHT.

The door opens. Eric comes in. Timid. Something shines in his hand.

          ERIC
    I'm sorry. I didn't mean
    to keep you waiting. I
    brought this…

He offers up a cleaver. The blade is polished and square. It looks ferocious.

          ERIC
    They're watching me now.
    At work. They saw how much
    I was taking. All for you…

A long pause. In the dark half of the cellar, the creature waits. Like it's listening. Like, impossibly… it understands him.

>   **ERIC**
> I couldn't tell them. How hungry you are. How much you need.
>
> …
> But we both know, anyway, that meat wouldn't have kept you… satisfied… for long.

He crumples onto the floor. His arm outstretched, all his fingers splayed out on the concrete.

All the skin and muscle of his forearm is gone, peeled off. The back of his hand is raw. Bone glints through the wet, sickly masses that throb at his wrist.

Eric looks up. The cleaver trembles in his raised hand.

ERIC
Please… don't make me do this.

The creature salivates.

Eric closes his eyes. Softly, the leaking pipe DRIPS.

ERIC
(whispering)
I was going to let you starve.

His eyes open. Red and puffy.

ERIC
I was going to ignore you. Leave you locked up down here, in the dark… let you die.

...
But I could <u>feel</u> you. You…

>   were inside my head. Why?
>   Why would you do that to
>   me? Make me feel all that…
>   hunger? All that pain?

His grip on the cleaver tightens.

>   **ERIC**
>   I guess you just wanted me
>   to understand.

The cleaver comes down. With a wet CHOK! it severs three of his outstretched fingers. Eric HOWLS.

Before the ragged stumps can even start to spurt blood, the creature's tongue whips forward and snatches the fingers off the floor.

Eric sobs. His moaning is interrupted by choked half-screams.

>   **ERIC**
>   God… oh, God… Jesus, fuck,
>   it… it hurts, fuck –

His eyes snap up suddenly. He shakes his head, as if replying to some silent comment.

ERIC
(whispering)
No.

...
You can't… still be hungry.

The cleaver topples out of his hand. He clutches at his bloody fingers.

Red streams gush down his arm.

The tongue smacks the concrete, inching and slurping towards the cleaver.

ERIC
No!

```
He realises his mistake. Goes to grab
the cleaver. But the tongue -
```

Dana jumped out of her skin. The door across the street slammed.

Quickly, she rushed to the kitchen window and looked outside. Condensation had gathered on the glass so she raised her wrist and wiped it away. Her eyes widened at the sight of the figure of the young man, heading away from her. Her Eric.

Instinctively, her eyes dropped to his hands. Damn it. She hadn't mentioned, in the script, which of his hands had held the blade and which had been mutilated. Or at least, she couldn't remember which it was now. She had assumed, for some reason, that his right had been the one on the floor, that he had raised the cleaver with the left –

And brought it down with the same –

But he was wearing gloves again. The snow had stopped falling, but the air was sickly and clung to him and so he had dressed in his blue parka and woolly hat and those thick, blood-red gloves, and sure, the fingers of the right hand looked a little deflated, but that didn't mean…

"Why would it?" she said softly. She wasn't writing reality. The young man was real. He was a real person, and he didn't have some monstrous thing in his basement. That was all her. Her inventions, her imaginations.

Thank Christ, she thought. Poor kid.

And her gaze tracked upwards, back to the back of his head. And she saw the bandage wound through his hair, just visible beneath the hem of his hat. Covering his right ear.

He was limping, still.

His ear, she thought. She smiled. Kid gets himself into some scrapes, huh?

The boy disappeared, and after a moment Dana moved to the kettle and poured herself a mug of coffee. She savoured it, still reeling drunkenly from her sleeplessness. She could feel the Dark Spot clearing from her mind, feel her sensitivities returning. Perhaps she could finish this screenplay, after all.

The screenplay, she remembered.

She left the mug on the counter and crossed swiftly to her little makeshift desk in the living room. Picked up the papers where she had left off. Wiping a spot of brown off her sleeve, she took the script into the kitchen and picked up the mug again. She heaved herself onto the countertop and read, picking up where she had left off:

```
He realises his mistake. Goes to grab
the cleaver. But the tongue snatches
```

it away and pulls it into the dark.

SFX: METAL DRAGGING OVER CONCRETE

          ERIC
No. Please…

He presses himself against the wall. Eyes filled with fright.

A beat –

And then the cleaver WOOSHES forward, slicing off his ear and burying itself in the drywall by his head. Blood explodes from the side of Eric's face. The tongue follows, enveloping the severed ear. It lingers…

And laps the blood off Eric's cheek, like a dog drinking water. The tip of the tongue worms into the ragged, red-cabbage mess left behind.

SFX: WET SLURPING

ERIC
Christ! God, why? Ah —
fuck, it hurts!

He staggers to his feet. The tongue lunges for the cleaver again.

Eric sees, in the corner of his eye, through a wash of blood. He whirls around, grabs for it —

And slips, curling his good hand around the sharp edge of the blade. He screams as it slices his palm. The tongue bats him away.

Something HISSES.

Eric turns, trying to wrestle the bloody cleaver out of the grip of the thrashing tongue. Tendrils of shadow flare in the dark.

He wins the weapon — snatches it away. Runs for the door, scrambling for the handle.

```
Another tongue - this one green and
slender - curls around his ankle,
yanks backwards. Eric falls, pulls
the handle down with him. The door
opens -

More     tongues.    Green,    yellow,
discoloured. Writhing and manic. He
crawls into the light, fighting them
as  they  grip  his  legs,  arms  -
shrieking, pounding at them -

And he makes it through. The door
slams behind him.
```

"His ear," Dana breathed, clutching the papers in her hands as if she were trying to squeeze the life out of them. The edges crumpled at her fingers. "Christ, his ear…"

She had known. Somehow, she had written about the young man's ear before she had seen the bandage wrapped around his skull.

Coincidence. It had to be. He was her inspiration… not the other way around. What she wrote, it wasn't true, wasn't real… couldn't be.

Was she making this happen?

Suddenly she threw the screenplay across the room,

disgusted. She was sick. Christ, she was *sick*. To think she could play with this boy's life – even on the pages of her stupid script – to think she could *use* him, or the idea of him, to fuel her own twisted fantasies…

And what if she had made them real?

"No," she murmured. She eased herself off the kitchen counter and gazed out of the window. "Don't be fucking crazy about this."

Her hands trembled. She steadied herself against the marble, hair falling in her eyes. Her gut twisted in knots, wrenching itself up into her chest. She felt sick.

No, she told herself. You can't remember writing that. Maybe you saw him, again – he must have already had the bandage on. That's what inspired that scene. You *saw* him, and you just… don't remember. You saw the bandage, and took inspiration – like you always do, from the smallest things in life – and you wrote that horrible, *fucking* thing…

She didn't feel sick, she realised. She felt hungry.

And when she closed her eyes, she could picture it so clearly. The cellar. The wall splashed with blood, the floor swilling with it. She was cold. Absent-mindedly, she reached up to close the window.

But it was already closed.

"You need to sleep," she whispered. Of course, she had slept for hours, but she felt exhausted. And her head… it pounded. Her mind scratched at the inside of her skull, clawing to get out. Confusion rattled her.

Everything was happening in the wrong order. Or *nothing* was happening, and she needed a fucking break. She glanced at the clock. Almost half twelve. Perhaps she could take a nap, get some writing in this evening before going to bed. She'd have no time for any of that tomorrow, not with a full shift at the Tea Barn. She needed to pee.

Her mind was racing. She looked down at the scattered pages and realised she couldn't sleep, not now. She had to know what happened next. She had to *write* what happened next.

But how was she supposed to know?

Frantically, she dove to the floor and gathered up the fragments of her script. Tried to rearrange them, shuffle them into some kind of order. All right, if this kid had finally gone as far as lopping parts of himself off for the beast in his cellar to eat… what would he do next? Cut off an arm? A leg?

No, he'd go backwards. The pain was too much. He was afraid. He'd retreat into old habits, try to find a more reasonable path.

That was it, she thought. That was logical. He'd try to steal again.

Better a criminal than a dead man, right?

"Oh, Eric," she whispered, and she bundled up the pages and clutched them to her chest. "What have I done to you?"

Nothing, she thought. I've done nothing to you. It's

not *real*.

Get a grip.

And she carried the screenplay over to her makeshift desk and sat. Her coffee had gone cold, so she left it. She was plenty awake, now, anyway. She had her next scene.

INT. BLACKWOOD BUTCHER'S SHOP - DAY.

The butcher's boy limps into the chiller, looking over his shoulder. A paper hat is pulled down over his ears. Or, where his ears should be. Tiny spots of red bleed through the material. He wears long sleeves and gloves beneath his apron.

With his good hand, he holds the rucksack. Open.

A fluorescent light comes on above his head and he moves to the shelves. Quickly, desperately, starts shunting joints and slabs of meat into his bag.

This is better. This is <u>enough</u>.

BLACKWOOD (O.S.)
Eric…?

Eric whirls around.

Blackwood stands in the door to the chiller. Disappointment ruins his face. Shame.

BLACKWOOD
I… I thought we were past this, Eric. I thought we were better than this.

ERIC
I… I wasn't –

Blackwood raises a hand.

BLACKWOOD
Save it, kid.

He hesitates. Frowns as his eyes drop

to Eric's arm. The limp fingers of the glove. Blood spreading beneath his sleeve.

        BLACKWOOD
Eric, what's going on? Why are you doing this?

Eric's jaw sets.

Hard.

He shakes his head.

        ERIC
You wouldn't understand.

        BLACKWOOD
I need to understand. Eric, I want to keep you working here. I like you, kid. But I can't… if you keep doing this. You know I can't. I have to let you go.

>   **ERIC**
>   No. Please, I…
>
> His face breaks suddenly. A single tear rolls down his cheek. The rucksack drops from his hand. Pain wracks his carved-up body, encased in shirts and gloves, hidden away.
>
>   **BLACKWOOD**
>   Eric, what's happened to
>   you? Why do you need… to
>   do this? Is it something
>   at home?
>
>   …
>   If you need help… if you
>   need me to get the police
>   involved…

Dana smiled, nodding to herself.

"That's it," she whispered. "That's the scene."

She cracked her knuckles and laid her fingers back onto the keys.

"And the butcher's boy says…"

> ERIC
>
> If you want to understand…
> you should come and see
> for yourself.

Blackwood raises an eyebrow.

EXT. SNOWY STREET – DUSK.

After closing, Blackwood and the boy walk to Eric's house. Their journey is hard, but short; soon they arrive at the pale green door.

Blackwood shoves his hands in his pockets as Eric fumbles, one-handed, for his keys. When he breathes out, his breath appears as mist.

It starts snowing again.

> **BLACKWOOD**
>
> What are we doing here,
> kid? If there's trouble,
> we should call the –
>
> **ERIC**

You'll see.

The door opens.

        ERIC
Come in.

INT. DANK CELLAR - CONT'D.

The door opens, slowly. It CREAKS.

Eric steps into the cellar. Turns his head.

        ERIC
Quietly. It… doesn't like strangers.

        BLACKWOOD
    (hissing)
It? What's going on, Eric?

Eric ignores him. Presses forward, into the dark. His eyes on the creature. Blackwood, behind him, hasn't seen it yet.

> **BLACKWOOD**
> I really think we should go -

Eric stoops to pick up the abandoned cleaver. The blade is covered in blood. He turns to the older man.

> **ERIC**
> I'm sorry…

Blackwood shakes his head.

> **BLACKWOOD**
> You're… Eric, what is this?

Suddenly a shape crashes out of the dark. Multiple shapes. Long, green tongues, a dozen of them. They coil and snap around Blackwood, throw him against the wall.

He screams.

Spines ripple on some of the tongues. Some, yellow, are wet and sticky. Thicker ones pin him to the drywall by his shoulders, by his stomach. One curls around the lower half of his face, muffling his screams.

          ERIC
    This is why I needed all that meat, boss. More than I could afford. <u>This</u> is why.

      ...
    Do you understand now?

Eric steps towards him, brandishing the cleaver. The butcher struggles. Thin, white tongues lap hungrily at him as others, like arms, restrain him with ease.

          ERIC
    And if you won't let me

take it…

Blackwood's eyes widen.

Eric lunges forward with the cleaver suddenly, swinging it at neck height.

The square blade buries itself in Blackwood's throat. His final scream is violent, terrible. The tongue across his mouth is drenched with red. More comes, bubbling out of his nostrils.

Eric GRUNTS, yanking the cleaver free. It didn't go all the way through. Blackwood twitches. Still alive, horrified.

Eric swings again –

And Blackwood's screaming stops as the blade swings through cartilage and bone and separates his head from his body. The tongues flail excitedly and let the body fall.

Eric smiles.

> **ERIC**
> Go on, then. Eat.

More tongues. Whipping out of the dark, curling around the corpse. Hungrily, they drag it into the dark.

SFX: CHEWING, SLURPING, TEARING

Dana had been writing for hours. She peeled herself away from the typewriter, stood up and stretched her arms.

"Christ," she yawned, looking up at the clock. It was barely six o'clock, but she felt she could quite easily fall asleep at her desk.

And she was so close to the end…

What end? she thought. That's it, surely. Our vulnerable, shrewy young man of a protagonist finally showed his true colours, finally turned to the dark side, stopped letting fear motivate him and started letting the *hunger*… and so, what else was there for him to do?

But she needed an ending.

It'll come, she thought, heading into the kitchen. The mug on the counter was cold, so she poured it out and put on the kettle.

She watched through the window as, across the street, amber-lit curtains flickered. Eyes narrowed, she gazed at the house with the pale green door and pulled up her stool.

Her attention shifted upwards as a dark shape moved on the second floor.

Eric looked out at her through an upstairs window.

For a long moment, they just stared at each other. And then the young man tugged the curtains violently across and disappeared.

"Shit," Dana said.

She sat at the window for hours, just watching. Long into the night, she waited. Nothing moved. She wondered if Eric would come out of the door at any point. Wondered if the butcher – Blackwood – would appear suddenly, unharmed. Wondered if he had ever been there.

And after a while, her head lolled forward and hit the counter, and she was asleep.

Dana slept heavily and dreamt, again, of the basement. She could almost feel the stifling cold of those concrete walls, the cloying dampness of it all. She saw shapes in the darkness, lazily writhing tongues that twitched and crawled and whipped up to the ceiling in desperate bids for the drips of water coming through cracks in the pipes and the cement.

She saw the butcher's carcass, almost completely stripped of meat, in one corner. Bundled over itself like a pile of fleshless, bony rags. Chicken bones, picked clean. One of his eyeballs remained in the socket, but the other was gone and half of his skull gazed blankly back at her through strips of pink muscle.

She could smell his blood on the air. Christ, she could almost taste him.

But he hadn't been enough. She was beginning to grow hungry again...

Something slammed on the cellar door. It swung open, closed again. Nothing came in. She froze, unsettled, unable to move. She listened.

Something was sneaking around inside the cellar. Something new. A visitor.

But she saw nobody. She heard the scraping of a chair over tiled floor. It sounded like the chair in her kitchen. She heard the clinking of mugs. A brief pause, and then the sound of another door opening.

She heard the tapping of typewriter keys.

No, she thought. That's my typewriter. Don't touch it...

Her eyes snapped open.

The kitchen was dark. Outside, snow pounded against the window and blotted out the moonlight. The swirling storm of snow was black and violent and she reeled back from it, almost toppling off her stool.

She whirled around. Something was different.

There was somebody in the house.

"Hello?" she said quietly, stepping off the stool. Her bare feet padded over the tiles. The chair that was usually tucked under the kitchen table had been pulled out. Somebody had sat in it... watching her. She wanted to shudder, but her joints were locked up, her muscles cold and stiff. Gingerly, she moved to the corner of the room and reached for the knife rack.

There was a creak from the living room.

Dana froze, the pads of her fingers trembling against the handle of a breadknife. Like the one in the script. The one Eric had used to shear long, pink rashers of flesh off of his shins and forearms. After a moment of silence, she unsheathed the knife and brandished it. The blade glinted steely in her hand.

Dana paused at the threshold of the kitchen, looking into the hallway. Without turning her head, she lifted her eyes and glanced sidelong at the front door. It had been pushed to, but she could see that the latch was up. Christ, had she left it unlocked?

Had she made it that easy for him to get in?

"Hello," she said, a little louder, tightening her grip on the knife handle. She looked back towards the kitchen. Everything felt wrong, out of place. Her heart throbbed in her ears, lids flickering as she tried to keep her eyes open. Closing them even for a fraction of a second – blinking – would make her vulnerable, make her easy prey. She had to stay alert, stay awake.

But how could she, with this *hunger* gnawing at her belly?

It was distracting, unbearable; it chewed at her stomach and made her sick. God, but she could feel him watching – now wasn't the time for distractions. She turned –

And saw him sitting at her desk. He was in the office chair, shuffling through papers. Her screenplay. He was reading her screenplay.

Dana opened her mouth. The only sound that came was a weak, hoarse moan.

He looked up from the script and smiled. His face was lashed by darkness, but she could see the whites of his eyes, the sickly pallor of his teeth. His chin was scarred by dermatitis, a thick rash of acne prevalent across his throat. His jaws were narrow and sunken. His hair – the strands that fell out from the rim of a red, winter hat – was unwashed and greasy.

Eric, she wanted to say, but that wasn't his name. That was the name she had given him. Oh god, he was right *there*.

He was going to kill her.

Dana said, simply, "You're in my house."

The space between two of her thudding heartbeats dragged on for an age, for what must have been most of the rest of her lifetime. She thought, what's he going to do to me?

She thought, shit, what's he going to *do* to me?

And then he blinked. "I'm so sorry," he said. His voice was lower than she'd imagined. "I didn't mean to – I just, the front door was open. I did knock, I didn't hear anything –"

"So you came in?" Dana asked, wide-eyed.

"I – okay, full disclosure," the young man said, raising both his hands over his head. "I was curious. I noticed you've been, kind of… watching me."

Dana swallowed. Guilt started to chew at her fear.

"Not in a weird way, I presume," he continued. "At least, I hope not…"

He left the sentence hanging, like a question. "Of course not," Dana said after a moment. She felt strange, defending her habits against a man who had invaded her home. Her grip tightened on the handle of the knife until her knuckles begun to whiten. "What are you doing in my house?"

"Honestly, I wanted to come and see if you were all right," he said. "I saw you in the window, a couple of times. You didn't look great. No offence."

He was still wearing gloves, she realised. Still dressed in the parka and blood-red scarf, winter hat pulled down over his ears.

"So I thought I'd come and check in on you. I don't know if you've left your house in the past week or—"

"I go to work," Dana said quietly.

"Okay. Anyway, I just wanted to come say hi, see if you were okay… and like I said, the door was unlocked. I couldn't hear anything. I didn't know if you might have... anyway, I saw that you were asleep, so I went to leave. I should never have come in, sorry. I don't know what I was thinking. But I should have left, then, and I... well, then I saw this."

He raised his hand. Dana couldn't tell if the fingers of his glove were filled in, or deflated and empty.

He was holding her script.

"I'm assuming this... guy... this is me, right? Eric?"

Dana nodded. "I just... I couldn't find any inspiration. Anywhere. You were a good life model. That's why I was..."

Her grip had loosened a little. He wasn't here to hurt her. But she wanted him to leave.

"How did you know my name?" the boy said.

Dana's blood ran cold. "I... what?"

He pointed at the first page. "You called your character *Eric*. A character based on... me. How did you know my name?"

"Your name's Eric?"

He cocked an eyebrow.

"I, uh... coincidence, I guess?"

"Hm."

"Look, could you—"

"Oh, yes. Yes. Sorry," Eric said, scrambling out of the office chair. He brushed his jeans down – again, Dana's eyes were drawn to his hand, and again, she just couldn't tell – and looked apologetically across the hall at her. He glanced at the breadknife. Dana didn't falter. He'd understand. The *creep*. "I'll be off, then. Sorry, for… you know."

Dana nodded. "I'll try to take it easy on the window-watching."

Eric laughed nervously. Christ, was he afraid of *her*?

"You know, if it'll stop you breaking into my house."

He nodded. "Right. Off I piss."

She said nothing as he stepped passed her into the hall.

He turned back, at the front door. "Why a butcher's shop?"

"What?"

"I work at a hunting range. Out of town. Halfway between here and Weeping. I'm guessing you saw *this*," he said, grunting as he lifted up the edge of his hat to reveal the gauze patch taped over his ear. "You wrote about it. I was just standing too close to a shotgun when it went off, is all. Blew out my eardrum."

Dana smiled thinly. She felt something like relief flood through her chest. For a moment, she had wondered whether, somehow, she'd been right about everything. About his name, his job, his injuries… about the thing…

"So, yeah," he said. "Why a butcher's shop?"

"Well, I guess... I know there's one close to here. Walking distance. And it worked for your story. You – the character, sorry, the character that I based on you – needed... the meat."

"For the giant monster in my basement," he grinned.

Dana grinned, too. "I know. Ridiculous, isn't it?"

"Oh, no, I've got one of those," Eric said. The grin disappeared. His eyes were stony and serious. "And she's still hungry..."

Dana opened her mouth. Nothing came.

Eric burst out laughing. The sound was unsettling. "God, your *face*!" he said.

"All right, now I need you to get out," Dana said, shaking her head. "Jesus. Do you do this to everyone you make eye contact with?"

"Only the ones who leave their front doors open." He paused again. "You know, your story – your script – kind of seemed unfinished. Are you working on an ending?"

"I am," she lied.

"Because if you're stuck... nah, don't worry. It's stupid."

"What?"

His hand hovered around the doorknob. He shrugged. "Well, you get your inspiration from real life, right? Real-life me turns into monster-feeding me. Real-life wound on my forehead turns into... well.

Maybe it would help if you were to come take a look around."

"Around what, your house?"

He shrugged again. "If it would help."

"That's okay," she said. "I'll leave the invasions of privacy to you."

Sheepishly, he scratched one-handed at the back of his neck. "Fair enough. Just thought, you know, if you needed to see the cellar, or anything... might help."

Dana paused. He might be onto something, there. She had been trying to find the spark of inspiration she needed for her ending for what felt like months now. Perhaps that was all she needed. Just to *see*.

"And I can make you a cup of coffee, order you a pizza or something," Eric said. "To apologise. You look like you could do with something."

She hesitated.

"I promise there's no monster."

"All right, sold," she said, nodding slightly. "This evening?"

"It *is* evening," he said.

"Oh. Now, then?"

"Now sounds good."

She raised the breadknife. "Let me just put this back and I'll be right along."

She followed him through the snow, hurrying through the pale green door with her head bowed as he held it open. In the thirty seconds it took them to cross the street, so many snow crystals had gathered in her hair that she felt drenched. She could feel them melting into her scalp.

Dana brushed her boots on a coarse doormat and kicked them off, hugging herself as the door slammed closed behind them.

"Brr," Eric said out loud, moving immediately to a thermostat on the wall. He dialled it up, with the same hand he'd used to scratch his neck, and gestured toward the inside of the house. "Coffee first, or straight to the cellar? Any inspiration yet?"

"Not yet," she shook her head. "Are you sure you're okay with this?"

"Least I can do," he said. "Come on, let's go right to the cellar." He led her through the hall and paused at a narrow doorway on the left.

"Down here?" Dana asked.

"Mm. Careful on these stairs. Have to admit, I don't go down here a huge amount, so it might be a shit-tip."

"It's nice," Dana said, looking around them. "Your place. How do you – if you don't mind me asking – how do you afford it?"

"Shared housing," he shrugged. "Students. Five of us."

Dana cocked her eyes to the ceiling. "Fair enough. Quiet lot, for students."

"Oh, they're not here," he smiled, pushing the door

open. "All in the process of moving out, actually. Place is about to get a lot more expensive."

"I see." She stepped past him, through the open door. A set of narrow, concrete stairs led down into the dark. Circular lights flickered faltering amber and yellow in the walls. Shadows climbed up from a second door, right at the bottom. Bolted shut.

"Feel anything? I don't know how this writing stuff works. What d'you get, like, a spark?"

She shrugged. "Honestly, I don't know if this'll work at all."

"Let's find out."

He overtook her on the narrow stairs, moving forward almost excitedly to unbolt the door at the bottom. As he ventured into the lowest third of the staircase, another disc of light flickered on overhead, momentarily blinding Dana. She paused, watched the young man limp down ahead of her.

The bolt came free with a heady, metallic scrape.

The door at the bottom of the stairs swung open.

Dana swallowed. "I'm not sure about this."

He turned his head, looked up at her. "It's just a cellar."

She shook her head. "I want to go home."

Eric's face hardened.

"I'm sorry. No offence. I just—"

She didn't get the chance to finish her sentence. Suddenly the young man was lurching up the stairs toward her, shadows licking his face. His eyes were dark, his jaw set, teeth gritted. He reached out.

"You're coming downstairs," he growled.

Dana staggered back, catching her heel on the step behind her. "No!" she cried. "Get away from me!"

He tried to grab at her throat. She lifted a hand to her face, instinctively curling her fingers around his. His glove came off in her hand. Fell to the ground.

She stared.

Eric's hand was a mess of raw skin. He only had two digits left – the thumb and index finger – and the others had been reduced to stubby, wet stumps. Bone jutted out of the wounds, and the flesh around his knuckles had begun to fuse into the muscle so that deformed lumps of red and pink knotted back from the injury and coursed into his wrist.

"Jesus…"

Eric swiped at her with the other hand and caught her hair, grabbed it. He pulled her down with him. Dana yelped, batting at him with both fists. He grunted, stumbled—

She took her chance and dived past him, hurtling for higher ground. She could smell blood.

"No!" he grunted. Something locked onto her ankle. He pulled, yanking her back. She tumbled.

Dana screamed as he plumbed his good hand into her hair and started to drag her down. "What the fuck are you doing?" she yelled.

He threw her down the last few stairs and lunged down after her, jamming his boot into her stomach before she could get back up onto her feet. He kicked her again, reaching up to remove the winter hat from his head.

He tore away the gauze patch and Dana saw just how badly his skull had suffered. His ear was missing, and in its place, a pipework of mangled tubes and twisted stems. Blood oozed slowly from the wound.

"It's all true," Dana breathed. "It all… how?"

Eric grinned, bending down to grab her by the shoulder and haul her to her feet. He shoved her into the cellar and stepped through after her. He smelled like death.

The door closed behind them.

"You know,' he began quietly, "a lot of research has shown that plants use electrical signals to communicate between the stem and the root. A little like us, I guess. Signals from brain to finger – back again, when you touch something hot – you know what I mean?"

There was something behind her, something in the dark, but Dana couldn't bear to turn around. She could sense it, feel the tremors of its sharp, whip-like tendrils scraping the walls all around her, hear it working its enormous, papery mouth…

"You work at the butcher's shop," she breathed. "You bring it meat. It's all *true*. How…?"

"There are theories," Eric said slowly, plunging his fingers into her hair. He smiled. "Some people think that plants can communicate with *each other*, through similar electrical signals. 'Nanomechanical oscillations'. That's what they call it. Tiny, *molecular* vibrations. They help each other to grow, influence each other through the electrical vibrations in the air between them. It's the closest thing to telepathic communication that we know of."

"And you think your plant's been communicating with... me?"

She felt hot breath on the back of her neck. Eric shrugged. "Who knows? She is rather a remarkable creature."

Dana felt hot tears stinging her eyes.

"Would you like to see her?" Eric said, twisting his fingers deep in her hair. He snatched back his wrist and she cried back at the pain.

"No. Please... I want to go home. I won't watch you again. I didn't mean... I never meant—"

"She wants to see you," Eric whispered.

Dana felt a tear escape her left eye. She could feel it in her head – or *something* in her head, something green and writhing – feel it behind her, reaching, spreading its jaws wide...

***

INT. CELLAR - CONT'D.

Eric leans in, digging his knuckles into the back of her head. Close shot of his face as his teeth flash.

> **ERIC**
> How's your ending coming along, you nosy bitch?

Dana shakes her head, desperate. Behind her, the shadow punches thick plant-like tentacles into the walls, twisting its great head.

Close on Dana's hand, behind her back, reaching into her jeans…

Eric pushes her back. The fringe-teeth of the plant creature quiver excitedly.

> **ERIC**
> I said, how's your ending—

"You tell me," Dana whispered, and she withdrew the breadknife from her jeans, yowling in pain as the serrated blade clawed its way up her thigh. Before Eric could look down she had jabbed upward with the knife and smashed the blade into his throat.

"Wh—"

He gargled as the blade drew neatly across his neck, splitting flesh easily. Blood winged across Dana's face and she gasped as warmth pattered the floor at her feet. "Fuck!" she yelled, taking a staggering step back as Eric crumpled at the knees, grasping at his neck with both hands. Blood pumped eagerly out through his fingers in glossy walls and his eyes went wide. Remembering the thing behind her, Dana wheeled past him, turning and planting a boot in his back, kicking him forward—

```
She  stares  as  the  plant  creature
lunges, mouth widening as blood fills
the stale air of the basement.


                  ERIC
            No… not me, eat her—


Dana screams as the creature envelops
him,  a  mass  of  fringe-toothed shadow
```

```
unfolding   and   closing   around   his
writhing body.
```

SFX: BONE BREAKS; CHEWING.

"Oh, Jesus," Dana moaned, stumbling back toward the stairs. "Oh, god, Jesus…"

She turned and lurched upward, scrambling for the banister. Behind her the creature swung its enormous head, pieces of Eric slopping out into a slimy fan that sprayed the floor and walls of the cellar. Halfway up, Dana stopped, glanced back over her shoulder. The breadknife was still clasped in her hand. She saw long green tendrils shooting out into the cellar, suckering to the walls as it fumbled hungrily in the dark. She felt a pang of… guilt? Sympathy? Something soft and painful in her stomach, something like pity. Or was that just the creature? Was it in her head right now?

Nanomechanical oscillations.

It couldn't be. No, this weird, squishy little feeling was her own. How long had the titanic flytrap been down here? How much longer could it survive, without anyone to feed it?

"Can you understand me?" she whispered.

The plant's body heaved below her, draped in shadows. She felt herself swallow. Had a little of Eric's blood ended up in her mouth? She could *taste* him.

Sickly, she found herself thinking – or found *something* thinking, inside her head – that he tasted pretty good.

ROLL CREDITS

Author's Note:

So this is an old one. Can you tell? And one that was very much inspired by a singular concept. After all, how can you write a new kind of story about a killer plant? From Charlotte Perkins Gilman to Arthur Conan Doyle, it's all been done. Right? To be quite honest, I'm not sure the inclusion of the 'telepathic' communications of plants was entirely original, either. But it was a hell of a lot of fun to write. I hope you enjoyed this one, too!

GOLD

(MY HOUSE IS AN ALLIGATOR)

The attic was locked.

There were enough problems with the new house that Rob scarcely found the time to look up, let alone consider the fact that there might be an entire storage space or even another bedroom up there. 116 Fern Street was subsiding, ever-so-slowly sinking into the ground – something that the surveyor had only discovered on his second assessment, three days *after* Rob had signed the preliminary contract – and among other things, trying to gauge the extent of the problem had kept him fairly busy for most of the week. Not only was the entire property destined to burrow its way into the earth within the next eighty years, but the kitchen desperately needed ripping out and replacing, and the upstairs bathroom was a wreck.

"Hi, love," he said wearily into the crook of his neck, bent up in the cupboard beneath the sink. The phone was crushed into the sweaty space between his cheek and his collarbone, and he could barely hear Hayley's voice through the erratic squawks of static in his ear. There was something about the service round here. Yet another fucking thing. "Yeah, I got your picture. I did. It looks great, love. You look beautiful."

He had asked about the attic when he'd first viewed the house, enamoured by the traditional brickwork fireplace in the lounge and the spacious bedrooms upstairs, and had received a fairly vacuous answer. Since then, he'd forgotten all about it. He'd sunk a good three-hundred grand into this place with the expectation of making three-fifty once the renovations were done.

"I am listening," he grunted, twisting the wrench in the dark space beneath the sink. With one eye closed he thrust his elbow into the corner of the cupboard, immediately gluing a clump of dusty cobweb to his cracked, red skin. "No, I mean it. It's a beautiful dress. And it doesn't—"

Another round of static buzzed in his ear and he sighed.

"—doesn't have to look exactly like your wedding dress, no, that's what I was saying. Yeah. Yeah, I know. Yeah. Okay, but we're only renewing our vows, we don't have to recreate…"

He closed his eyes as a bright bolt of pain crisscrossed the back of his skull. He had another migraine coming on.

"Listen, love, I think you're beautiful. Really. Always. And it's a really nice dress. No, I… no, I didn't mean 'only' renewing."

He backed up out of the cupboard, stifling a yelp as he reared up too quickly and smashed the top of his head on the frame. Clamping a hand down over the sore spot he stumbled back into the kitchen, looking out onto the street. The houses across the road were little more than vague silhouettes in the fading sun, boughs of gold tinging the bottoms of deep pink clouds. The sun was already slipping away from him.

"I love you too, sweetie," he said. "Not long now, all right? I promise I'll be done with this shithole in a few weeks, and then I'll be more helpful with all the invitations and—oh. I didn't realise you'd done it, I'm sorry. Yeah. Yeah, I will. All right. Bye."

He turned around, rubbing the crown of his head as deep throbbing waves of agony swelled through the spongy tissue of his brain.

116 was a bit of a fixer-upper, but it shouldn't have been anything he hadn't dealt with before. He'd made calls to all the right contractors, lined up a couple potential buyers before he'd even started work – this should have been a six-month job, tops. Six months' work, a few hundred cups of coffee, and thirty-thousand dollars profit. Easy.

If only the damn house wasn't caving in like everything else around him.

***

Rob stood at the bottom of the stairs with his *White Buffalo* cap wedged on his head and a steaming mug of coffee in his hand. His shirtsleeves were rolled up past the elbows and his arms caked with grease, knuckles flashing white through the cracked smudges of oil on his hands. The knees of his overalls were stained green. He had momentarily zoned out as he wandered absent-mindedly from the kitchen to the staircase, and as he tipped the mug up to his mouth to drink, his eyes flitted to the ceiling.

The hatch was embedded in the plasterwork, the wood and frame pale-white and almost indiscernible from the rest of the ceiling; were it not for the brassy glint of the padlock, he would not have registered that he was looking directly at it.

"Huh," he murmured, lowering the mug. Around him, a mess of flaky plaster pieces and shredded scraps of wallpaper littered the hallway floor. The carpet had been torn up and the floorboards beneath were rough and pale. Here and there tiny nails poked up through the wood.

Setting his coffee on the floor, Rob reached into his overalls for the hammer swinging against his hip. He withdrew it, his eyes still on the hatch. A long-handled claw hammer, its head speckled with rust.

Climbing up to the landing, he retrieved a stepladder from the bedroom and unfolded it, placing it directly beneath the hatch and struggling up onto the top step. His big feet clumsily balanced on the step, a sudden surge of vertigo nearly sending him backward.

Without sparing the padlock a glance, Rob punched the hammer upward and smashed the head right into the bolt to which the glinting brass thing had been attached. There was a sound like the ricochet of a bullet in one of his dad's favourite Clint Eastwood movies and the bolt keened into itself, folding into a right angle. This sound was followed by the dull tinkle of the padlock hitting the rungs of the stepladder as it fell, then the *thwump* of it sinking into the carpet.

Gingerly, Rob tucked the hammer into his overalls and reached up to push open the hatch.

It was a phenomenal effort to haul himself up into the attic, and he was out of breath when he finally bundled his legs over the edge and rolled onto his back. Only now did he realise that it was almost entirely dark up here, the only light coming from down below; slowly he sat up, giving his eyes time to attune to the pitch. Eventually he made out the thin snag of a frayed cord hanging above the open hatchway, and he leaned forward to tug it sharply.

Light exploded into the attic and flickered. Dull blossoms of amber washed the rafters.

Rob crouched awkwardly, immediately deflating

when he saw that the attic was only half the size of the bedroom and about a third of the height; indeed the rafters slanted in ward at such an angle that even perched on his ankles right in the middle of the loft, his head thumped the ceiling. So much for a third bedroom. In fact, he thought, blinking as the flickering light assaulted his eyes, there wasn't much room for storage either: even the previous owner had only left a couple boxes here, stuffed against the back wall.

Curious, he crawled around the hatch and fought his way toward the boxes. He was acutely aware that the day was running away from him again, but there were only so many hours per day that he could waste deciding whether to spend a few more thousand dollars on resin injections and underpinning or just try and convince the buyers that the place would still be standing when they retired. A minute away from it all wouldn't hurt.

He spent far longer than necessary trying to pick away the tape securing the first box before deciding to rip the lid off instead. Inside were a selection of porcelain mugs and figurines, carefully wrapped in newspaper. He tucked them back in, largely disinterested in the contents but aware that even stuff like this could be worth something; crockery was more Hayley's forte. He'd have to call her this evening and ask her about the mugs.

The second box was more difficult to open;

whoever had stored them up here – presumably the same person who'd locked the attic – had taped all around the corners and edges so that he had to spend a full ten minutes gradually ruining his nails in an attempt to get inside. Eventually he found a lip in the tape casing and worked his way in.

More newspaper. He sighed softly, expecting more figurines. Still, what was he hoping for? A few grand bundled up nicely? A couple gold bars?

Digging into the newspaper, he recoiled as his hand brushed something cool and wet. "What the—"

No.

Not wet, he realised, wiping his hand on his overalls. *Scaly*. More cautiously this time, he poked at the newspaper and burrowed a small hole until he could see what was hidden inside. Polished leathery scales glittered in the dim light of the attic: he caught a glimpse of a yellowed, serrated tooth. A flash of gold.

"Holy balls," he whispered.

The kitchen was a mess. The cupboard doors were gone, exposing the hollowed-out cavities beyond; the tiles had been ripped up and the new tiling had only begun to creep out from one corner in the past few days, forgotten as he spent hours on the telephone with contractors who told him, time and time again, exactly what he already knew: that by the time they were through with the underpinning, the house on Fern Street would have cost him more than he could afford to lose.

He cleared the table quickly, shunting everything onto the floor and planting the thing from the attic right in the middle of the new, hastily-polished space. Now Rob stood in the kitchen doorway, staring into its eyes. His stomach twisted nervously as it stared back.

As far as he could tell, the thing was real.

It was enormous, but still he got the feeling that it had only been a juvenile when it had been killed. There was a shallow black scorch-mark between the ridges around its eyes that he imagined was the carefully-treated scar of a gunshot wound. Tiny, almost imperceptible stitched around the stump of its neck, sealing the polished bone and stuffing inside.

It was disgusting.

His guts turning with revulsion, Rob reached for the phone in his pocket and dialled quickly. Holding it to his ear, he kept his eyes on the thing and swallowed.

After a moment, he hung up.

Take a moment, he thought. *Really think about this, before you do anything stupid.*

The alligator head watched him, its might jaws split open by a cruel, ululating grin.

It was three times the size of his own head, with a great flat snout exploding into a mess of smashed ivory teeth. The lips and gums were a pale, sickly yellow, the inside of the mouth a black hole. The leathery skin was ridged and spiky in places, such a dark emerald that it was almost black too. Flared nostrils were framed by frilled horns; the paler scales of the thing's lower jaw and neck were smooth and speckled with brown.

Its eyes had been removed and replaced with two perfectly-spherical balls of solid gold.

Each was an inch and a half across and sunk perfectly into the spiny mounds of the thing's brow, glinting viciously in the light of the kitchen. Some of the teeth had been replaced too, and little curved spears of shining yellow protruded from the thing's stuffed, leathery gums as though they had grown there naturally.

A beat, and then Rob lurched for the kitchen counter. Swiping aside a couple of empty takeout containers he fumbled for the cutlery drawer, digging around inside with a dreadful rattle before clamping his fingers around a plastic-handled teaspoon. Whirling around, he faced the grinning alligator head and swallowed.

"This won't hurt a bit," he said, and he surged forward.

Gritting his teeth, Rob clamped one hand down on the alligator's skull, right between the eyes where the bullet had entered its brain. With the other he poked forward with the teaspoon, thrusting it into the tiny sliver of black between the first golden eyeball and the scales that erupted into irregular whorls around it. There was a wet slithering sound and the teaspoon curved around the back of the gold ball. With a grunt, Rob slammed the heel of his hand forward—

The alligator's golden eye flew out of the socket, punching into the wall behind him and dropping to the floor, where it rolled between his feet. Triumphantly Rob grinned, bending down to pick it up.

The house trembled.

He froze, doubled over with his fingers splayed around the gold ball. For a moment he thought he must have imagined it in his excitement, but then the house shuddered a second time.

An earthquake?

Now?

Rob grabbed the golden eyeball and straightened up, slipping it into his overalls. His eyes moved to the window above the sink: outside, the low rooves of the houses across the road were still. Number 116 was still. He *had* imagined it.

His attention dropped to the alligator head and he balked.

A steady stream of gluey, bright red drizzled from the empty eye-socket he had raided.

He could swear the thing's grin had widened a little.

***

Rob slept uneasily on the mattress in the smaller bedroom, eight inches off the carpet and tucked awkwardly into a striped Lifesavers sleeping bag. The house would be sold unfurnished, of course, but he regretted not ordering a cheap bedframe for his temporary living quarters. Every day that he grew more deeply involved in the chaos that was saving Number 116 from the ground, he became more certain that he never should have bought the damn place; all his buyers had backed out, and even the contractors he'd hired seemed reluctant to do work around here for anything less than the asking price of the property itself. What the hell was it about Fern Street that made people so goddamn *scared*?

He woke up a little after midnight to the sound of slithering in the bedroom wall.

Rob's eyes snapped open. The room was dark, only the faintest halo of moonlight filtering in through the blinds and dappling the carpet with spangles of dim grey-blue. His skin was drenched in sweat and he shivered as he instinctively grabbed for the sleeping bag, tightening the casing around him. For a full minute he lay there, groggy and half-dazed, wondering if the sound that had woken him up had been a part of his dream.

Another minute passed, and the wall shuddered again.

Rob bolted upright, wheeling as the mattress sagged

beneath him. The sound was like something enormous and long snaking through the cavity in the wall: he heard the scuffling of rats amplified by a thousand, and then the *smack* of a long, leathery tail against a supporting iron rod. He turned his head to look in the direction of the sound but it was moving fast: before he could pinpoint the location of the thing in the walls it had scuttled toward the landing and disappeared.

Silence.

"What the fuck…"

Rob heaved himself out of the sleeping bag and staggered half-blind across the room, his boxers clinging to him, grey tee soaked with sweat. Rubbing grit out of one eye, he paused on the landing and listened. A few beats passed, and he realised he was swaying gently, his legs fatigued from the day's work.

Nothing. He had imagined it. "Oh, for fuck's sake," he whispered, turning around to get back into bed. He paused, realising he needed to relieve himself and deciding instead to head for the bathroom. Might as well, while he was up. He'd only have to go in a couple hours anyway.

As he turned for the bathroom, something scuffled in the wall across from him. His head snapped round and he followed the wet, slithering smacking sound as it boomed across the stairs. There was something moving in there; it dragged itself loudly downward and he lowered his gaze, following it down, down to the entrance hall…

"No," he muttered. Jesus Christ, on top of everything else… was he really going to have to call in pest control?

He thundered down the stairs, following the sound toward the front door. Here it paused before the thing in the walls careened in the opposite direction, heading past the kitchen and lounge to the small downstairs bathroom. It was larger than a rat, that was for sure. moving like a snake, its body scraping the edges of the crawlspace as it sluggishly ploughed through the plaster.

"Are you shitting me?" Rob called angrily, refusing to acknowledge the fact that the rat-cum-badger-cum-elephant in the walls probably couldn't understand him. "I'm renewing my vows in a fucking week and I need this house *done*, you hear me?"

The sound stopped.

The house was still; only now did he realise that it had been trembling around him. Quickly he moved into the bathroom, sharply tugging the cord to turn on the light. Cringing as it flooded the room, he surveyed the walls, breathing heavily.

The thing was gone.

Well, fuck it. As long as that thing – whatever it was – kept quiet while the realtors were showing buyers around, he could deal with it.

***

In the morning, he pried loose the second golden eyeball and the rest of the teeth. Wrapping the lot of them in a sandwich bag and tucking it into his pocket, he drew in a deep breath and locked eyes with the defiled alligator head on the kitchen table. It stared blankly back at him.

There must have been a pound and a half of gold in that sandwich bag. If it was solid, like he thought, then…

Well, then everything would be different.

"Back in a while, crocodile," he quipped dully, then he swiped his keys from the table and turned to leave for the jewellers'.

Rob was halfway across the drive when he saw the monster in the backseat of his car.

"What the…"

He froze, the keys for the old Jazz gripped tightly in one hand. Within moments the knuckles had turned bone-white but he didn't notice, his gaze locked on the rear window of the little hatchback.

Bright hungry eyes looked back at him from inside, the piercing yellow scarcely dulled by the greasy rheum coating the glass. The shape curled up in the backseat was enormous and somewhere in the terrified goop of his brain a voice screamed out that this insane thing was real, it had to be, because the weight of it had made the back of the car sag right down onto its axles so that it was almost scraping the tarmac. As it reared up its head the hatchback's suspension jounced with an awful squealing sound. The creature was a titan of black scales and ridged, bumpy spines, its tail slung over the headrest of the driver's seat, its jaws puffing great blooms of vapour onto the inside of the window.

The creature grinned, flashing dozens of sharp white points.

Rob cursed under his breath.

Then the beast's gargantuan snout ploughed forward and the window shattered, a great bellowing roar exploding from the darkness inside the car. Rob staggered backward, awkwardly fumbling for the front door key as a spray of glass and scales showered the tarmac. The car tipped forward and the shape slithered out through the ragged hole, jaws clamping shut hard and then opening wide, impossibly wide, head swinging from side to side as thunder rumbled in its throat—

Eyes locked on the beast's impossible maw, Rob scrambled for the lock and the door swung open, nearly dragging him onto his butt in the hallway. The alligator thrashed its tail as it crashed onto the drive, smashing a great volcanic dent into the side of the car, then it was moving toward him, slamming its enormous claws into the tarmac and propelling its low, black body forward.

The door slammed shut just as the creature snapped its jaws. Rob yelped as it punched into the wood behind him and the whole front wall of the building shuddered. "Fuck!"

He scrambled for the nearest window and yanked back the curtains, almost slamming his face into the glass as he looked desperately outside.

Nothing there.

The car was empty, the window unbroken. There were no shapes in the backseat – nothing on the drive, either, though he could smell the dank swamp-water that coated the creature's spiny back, the thick ripe meaty scent of its breath…

"What the fuck is happening?" he breathed, glancing at the door. He could have sworn the weight of the beast had splintered the wood panels into ruins.

The door was untouched.

Rob hunched over the toilet bowl, the acrid taste of bile in his mouth, his stomach churning violently. His skin felt cold and clammy and the hands that gripped the edges of the bowl were pale. He could almost see tinges of blue in his nailbeds.

Nothing else came up, his stomach having emptied itself fully in the last half hour or so. Wearily he eased himself into a half-standing position then, unable to sustain that for more than a minute, plonked his rear onto the toilet seat.

There was a gurgle from the water beneath him. Almost imperceptible, like the minute sound of a tadpole swimming about in the bowl. He didn't notice.

Absent-mindedly Rob reached into his pocket, searching for his phone. It was probably about time to give Hayley another call. Tell her that he'd be coming home this weekend. Whether the house was finished or not, he wanted out of here. They could push back the sale for a while; wasn't like anyone was biting

(*ha*)

anyway. And so what if they couldn't afford to go on the second honeymoon they'd planned? Hawaii had been great the first time, but right now all he could really remember was the awful fever he'd gotten from the food.

Another gurgle from deep within the U-bend, a meaty belch that sent ripples through the water.

Rob's fingers brushed the sandwich bag in his pocket and he paused before digging it out. Inside, two golden balls and a collection of twenty-four-karat teeth, jostling against each other as he massaged the bag in his hands. They shone brightly in the unpleasant bathroom light.

Was this the problem? Had he messed with something he didn't understand?

"Don't be a fucking idiot," he murmured, shoving

the gold pieces back into his pocket.

Inches from his rump, something thin and dark grinned in the toilet bowl. A juvenile, its face narrower and paler, its eyes no less hungry.

"You're just tired," he whispered, clamping his hands over his temples. "Tired of this fucking house, this fucking street, tired of fucking *life*, you're not—"

A sudden bolt of movement as he stood up, face flashing red with anger. Absent-mindedly he reared back to slam his hand down on the flush. The explosion of water in the toilet satisfied him somewhat, though he didn't see the dark, wide-jawed shape slipping back down the U-bend, retreating with its long, slender tail coiled around its claws.

"Get off your butt," he told himself a little redundantly, "and sort yourself out. You're going crazy, that's all."

He turned to the sink and screamed as it exploded off the wall, the long jaws of an alligator hatchling snapping around his wrist as its slim, black body shot out of the tiles in a gush of hot, swampy water. The sink smashed into the bathtub as a bright hot pain shot up his arm and Rob staggered back, eyes widening in horror as another hatchling, slightly bigger than the first, slithered out of the gaping crack in the tiles. Then came a third – and a fourth – and finally he ripped his eyes away from the black hole in the wall and looked down at the creature clamped to his arm. He batted it into the wall and the thing squealed as its teeth slid out of his skin and it fell onto the cistern tank, setting off the toilet's flush again.

"Jesus *fuck*!" Rob yelled in agony as a thick network of glossy red webs spread across his arm. Stumbling for the door, his foot keened through a spreading pool of water and something bit down into his calf, sending another shooting pain up his leg as it tore away a warm chunk of flesh. Behind him more and more alligators slithered through the hole where the sink had connected to the wall: a dozen of them – two dozen – flooding the bathroom and sliding about in the spray of sewage that followed, snapping their jaws as they scuttled after him. quickly Rob jammed down the handle and tumbled out into the hall, turning to look back as he kicked the door shut. In that frantic half-second he saw that the bathroom had filled with black, spiked shapes, that the tiles had teeth and the bathtub was crawling with snapping grey animals—

Rob screamed, slamming his back into the door. His leg trembled, threatening to buckle beneath him. How many pints of blood before he went into medical shock? Was he there already? Was this whole thing a hallucination?

Mania pumping through his veins, Rob hurtled forward. He had to get out of the house, at least get onto the street—

A black shadow fell over him and he looked up.

"Oh, Jesus Christ almighty," he whispered.

***

The ceiling was a rippling vortex of black scales and deep, half-healed slashes. Smears of pale flesh bulged between bloated ridges of leathery green and dozens of winking reptilian eyes watched him from within the swirling, contorting mess, the walls popping and ripping open as plaster blackened and turned to leather. Behind him he heard the bone-shattering thumps of dozens of tiny creatures punching their bodies into the bathroom door. The carpet squelched wetly beneath his feet; the gushing water from the exploded sink had begun to seep into the house.

Rob whimpered and lurched for the front door, recoiling when it swung open and flashed its teeth. The outside was gone – Fern Street was gone – and all he could see through the mouth-shaped doorway was the deep, red tunnel of a scarred, ancient throat and a knotted mass of lashing, wet muscle that he could only assume was the great throbbing tongue of the beast.

Wheeling away, he glanced toward the bathroom door and saw that the creatures had started to break it down, tiny snapping jaws poking through great ragged wedges in the wood. "Fuck," he whispered, starting for the stairs.

The carpet clawed at him as he grabbed for the

banister. He tried to wrench his hand loose as the cool scales of reptilian skin brushed his palm but it was too late: an impossibly long coil of ribbed, black tail snapped tightly around his wrist and pinned him to the newel post.

"What do you want from me?!" he yelled, yanking his whole body back to withdraw his arm from the banister rail's grip. His eyes shot up to the landing and he moaned as he saw that the bedroom door was open; inside, an enormous, scaled shape writhed off his mattress and started toward the landing.

There was only one thing he could do.

As he lunged for the kitchen the hallway buckled beneath him, the great ribs of some impossible beast splaying like the hood of a cobra and shunting the floorboards apart. The whole house was spinning now, subsiding into the earth a good few decades too soon, and as he threw himself toward the kitchen door his left side smashed into the frame, enveloping his bones with a thick coat of pain. "I'm giving them back!" he pleaded desperately, fumbling in his pocket as he staggered into the kitchen. "For god's sake, I'm trying to give them back, if you'd just *let* me—"

He froze.

The kitchen was a great black maw, hundreds of thousands of smashed, white teeth bursting out of the fleshy walls. Swamp-water pooled over the tiles, each one now a rubbery, black-green scale shivering with hungry anticipation. The table was still there, but it was covered in spines and sinking into the fleshy muscle of the alligator tongue beneath.

And the head was gone.

"No…" he moaned, the gold eyeballs heavy in his hand. The alligator head had disappeared. His only hope.

A titanic hand clamped down on his shoulder and Rob screamed. Another twisted into his thinning hair and he realised they weren't hands, not really – they were claws. Enormous, lengthened alligator claws.

Slowly, he turned around.

The beast grinned down at him, half of its teeth missing, its eyes gone and the deep, sunken pits of the sockets bruised and purple. Its body was gargantuan, the smell of its breath fruity and rotting.

"I'm sorry," Rob said. "I'm so sorry. I let you down, I know that. I never meant… please know that I never meant to let you down. Not once. This isn't what I'd planned on saying, god knows it isn't, but… please… please know that I never meant to hurt you. Please."

The blind beast's gruesome smile widened as the blind, wide-faced creature leaned forward and bumped Rob's forehead with its snout. A long, purple sliver of tongue drew a wet path across his face.

"*Your apology is… lacking,*" the monster rasped hungrily.

"I know," Rob whispered, "but it wasn't for you."

Rob closed his eyes and hung up the phone in his hand.

As the creature's teeth began to close around his head, he prayed that Hayley would find the money somewhere to take herself on that second honeymoon they'd been planning.

Author's Note:

Here's the second story in this collection which has been previously published, this time by the fantastic TerrorCore Publishing in their first anthology, Doors of Darkness. *This story was written for a specific prompt (albeit one that really allowed me to do whatever I liked with it) and I remember writing it without knowing much of what was about to happen before it happened. But I knew there'd be an alligator with a golden eyeball, and I knew some nasty things might happen when that eyeball was removed (as it is bound to be). Isn't that all you need, sometimes?*

CORAL

Christmas. 2006.

The kitchen was smoking.

April Leek would always remember how quickly the sweet, chewy, honeylike smell of roasted parsnips had turned to an acrid charcoal-menthol blossom that had clogged the air and filled her lungs. She was only five at the time, but the images that replayed in her head every December were crisp and powerful, unrelenting. She remembered, clear as day, the cornucopia of shrill moans as Uncle William crashed drunkenly into the Christmas tree and smashed half the ornaments on the living room wall (they had called him the Billdozer ever since). She recalled the grimace on Nana's face as three faceless eight-year-old cousins (they were all as bad as each other) scrambled around her feet, scuffing the carpet as they played tag and rolled into the skirting boards. Remembered the repugnant, disgraceful scrabbling at the table as everybody tried to grab the same oily handful of goose.

She remembered the terrible and absolute mental

breakdown that her mother had had, and the arduous series of separations and divorces that had finally irreparably severed her parents' marriage in the spring of 2009.

April's father had decided sometime after that Christmas that they wouldn't have family round again. Not all of them at once, anyway. Nana could have Christmas, and Uncle William and his repugnant kids could come over for Easter, as long as there was no booze in the house. April's great grandfather (April's mother's grandfather, who had little pockets of peppery freckles hammered into the wrinkles either side of his nose) came to visit on July 4th, having decided that he would celebrate any damn holiday he pleased in his old age, despite being staunchly and definitely British.

Aunt Coral came to see them at Halloween.

Any other holiday, April and her dad would have been fine. They'd never have known. If only April's great-aunt Sam hadn't been such a pagan and insisted on visiting the Leeks on the Spring Equinox, maybe they'd have made it to November unscathed.

But that was the way it was.

October fumed with orange light and sprinklings of ink-black cloud. Every night that passed grew a little darker and a little longer, the fields blooming with misshapen orange gourds as kids became restless and unhinged.

April Leek was seventeen. Too old for trick-or-treating, but not old enough to be excused from the whole thing. Her father still expected her to get excited about picking a pumpkin to carve, and still laughed whenever she cringed at the feeling of the gooey, cold strings inside. He had started to criticise the artistic definition of her carvings, now that she was old enough to know what she was doing with a knife. At a certain point after April's sixteenth birthday, Ron Leek had tried explaining to his daughter that pumpkin pie could be both a sweet and a savoury treat, and she'd promptly threatened to shove his head in one and see *then* how he felt about dessert.

They argued a lot nowadays.

The air was cold and spiced with notes of lime and frosty earth. April gritted her teeth as she stepped lightly off the bus and slung her backpack over a sore shoulder, her whole body aching from hockey practice, her left shin particularly bruised from one midgame assault. Her gym clothes and books smacked her hip rhythmically as she walked, the bus pulling away with a gassy, pneumatic hiss and overtaking her in a wobbling spray of yellow. Her gaze drifted across the road as she walked, her Docs clicking on the pavement.

The Chamberlains had dressed their front lawn with streamers of blood-red and visceral pink, the clipped grass scattered with orange confetti. A six-foot plastic skeleton hung over the porch, its bony hands dangling hooks upon which buckets of sweets had been hung. They wobbled in a gentle breeze, a laminated sign on the fence advertising their availability in dripping bloody letters. Next door to the Chamberlains, number sixty-four had planted two intricately carved pumpkins beside the fence, one a tall squash-like affair with the Calusari from the *X-Files* snicked into its flesh; the other was short and plump, and a bloated caricature of a savage grizzly bear had been cut so expertly that orange layers of varying thickness would produce different amounts of glaring yellow light when the candle inside was ignited.

Her eyes turned toward home as she neared the end of the street. She froze.

There was a hearse parked on the kerb right outside number seventy-one.

April stood staring at the vehicle for a full minute, a surprising number of morbid possibilities racing through her head. The hearse was ancient, a long pale-blue thing with wings and cream highlights. It was majestic in a way, the polished windows around the back exposing a deliciously plus, crimson interior, the curtains tucked into their frames a gloriously rich purple.

She swallowed, realising quickly that if somebody she knew had died, the vehicle parked on the pavement would far likelier be an ambulance than a hearse. That could only mean one thing.

October 29th.

Aunt Coral had arrived.

April stepped tentatively inside and dropped her rucksack on the doormat, scraping her shoes quickly before kicking them off. The hallway smelled meaty. There was a thick, cloying muddiness to the air that reminded her of the rotting deer carcass she and Stacey Hipperson had found in the woods one week after college. Every day that week they'd returned to the woods to see if somebody had taken it away. Nobody had, and every day it smelled a little worse. Blue fuzz began to creep into the dark pits around its eyes and the bright splashes of entrail spilling from its belly crawled with tiny black flies.

"Daa—aaad!" she called, edging into the hallway. "I'm home!"

Waiting for a response from her father, she noted the long, black cloak hung on the coatstand. The polished, pointed heels tucked underneath. The wide-brimmed black hat crowning the newel post of the long, narrow staircase leading up to her bedroom and her father's. The cloak was made of some papery, lace-like material with swirling patterns of velvet stitched into it; the hat was like something a plague doctor would wear.

The shoes were nice enough.

"*Dad!*" she yelled, stepping toward the open kitchen door. "You here?"

There was a sniff from the kitchen and April paused. Every fibre in her body stiffened, crackling with anticipation. Summer had only recently swapped shifts with autumn, and Ron Leek suffered horrendously from hayfever. She *knew* his sniff.

"Aunt Coral?" she called eventually, her voice breaking.

Nothing for a few seconds. And then, fizzing as if through a speaker: "*Hello, dear...*"

April steeled herself and moved toward the kitchen, opening her mouth as she stepped over the threshold. "Hel—"

There was a gust of musty air and Aunt Coral appeared in the doorway, looming over her. April blinked, almost taking a staggering step back before she realised she hadn't actually *seen* the old woman teleport across the room.

"Hi," she said timidly, suddenly feeling like she was five years old again. That fateful Christmas, Aunt Coral had just sat at the end of the long, long table and watched it all unfold, occasionally sipping from a mug of earl grey that never seemed to empty. Peeking over the woman's shoulder into the kitchen, April saw that it was otherwise empty. "Is my dad about?"

Aunt Coral was a mountain despite the hunched crook of her spine – the top of which bulged out of her back like a melon-sized tumour – and she almost completely filled the doorframe even without her wide plague doctor's hat. She leant forward on a spindly gnarled walking stick, the handle a knot of interlocking white roots carved into an explosion of flapping feathered wings, in which her long, bony fingers rested quite comfortably. Like a clump of angular, white-knuckled worms knifing through each bird's wooden back.

"No, dear," she said softly, the wind whistling through her teeth, each of them long and thin and yellow, pointed inward from her gums so that her narrow mouth was like a cave entrance stuffed with stalactites and stalagmites. She was dressed all in black, her long curved body pinned into the shadowy folds of a velvet blouse, her legs swallowed by a long, inky skirt. "I'm afraid your father… had to run. Asked me… to let you know he'd… be back soon."

Every sentence was punctuated with long, whistling breaths that seemed to wrack the old woman's lungs terribly. As she spoke, April assessed the jewelled brooch pinned to her aunt's breast (a small circular stained-glass design bedazzled to give the impression of a tiny red man presenting something long and sharp and black to a flame-haired woman in all green) and the necklace that swung from her withered throat, a string of gold marble-sized baubles with odd symbols laser-cut into them. Aunt Coral's hands were decorated with a collection of rings, perhaps seven or eight in total.

It was only after a moment had passed that April realised that a) she hadn't heard a word Aunt Coral had said, and b) she had spent the past minute trying not to look up into the old woman's eyes. Slowly she did, tilting her face upward until she met Coral's face. "I'm so sorry," April said, "what did you say?"

Aunt Coral smiled thinly. Her nose was a pointed, vulture-like beak, her hair greasy-grey and pulled tightly back from a forehead sprinkled with liver spots.

Her eyes were rheumy pools of pink-white that seemed to glow wetly in the light of the kitchen. Pupilless and blank, they nonetheless bored right into April's soul, seeing the impossible despite the old woman's blindness.

"Your father… will be home… later," Aunt Coral whispered.

Monday night, April realised. Her dad had driven across town to a meeting. Every Monday, Wednesday, and Thursday he attended a small AA circle in the Orthodox Church building and on Saturday morning he ran a meeting of thirty-or-so people via Zoom. They were some of his best friends.

Well, at least he'd be back soon.

"Say… dearie," Aunt Coral croaked, her thin lips

stretching, and April noticed tiny rivets and cracks in the skin around her mouth. Red-raw bumps at her temples, splotches of pepper-yellow around her eyes. "Would you mind... helping your auntie get... her things upstairs?"

It was like she was trying to beat her own personal best for how-many-words-can-I-fit-in-before-the-next-wheeze. She was painful to listen to. And there was something swimming in those eyes...

"No problem," April said, hoping it at least sounded like she was smiling. "You're in the spare room, right?"

"Your father said I could have... the attic..."

April cocked an eyebrow. "You want the attic? There's a ladder and everything—"

"I... insisted," Aunt Coral said, her fingers tightening on the knotted murmuration of tiny, carved birds that made up the head of her cane. Giant bony worms strangling their prey mid-flight. "Please... my bags."

"Sure," April said. She glanced back toward the stairs and saw that a fat black duffel bag and a bulging, snakeskin handbag had been dumped on the third step. "You wait here, all right? I'll go take it up."

"Aren't you a dear," Coral whispered. Leaning close, she let out a long, slow sigh and April felt hot meaty breath waft into her throat. Resisting the urge to cringe, she nodded slightly. Aunt Coral inhaled, then spoke again. "I could just… eat you."

April backed up, heading slowly for the stairs without taking her eyes off the crone's withered, birdlike face.

"I think this is going to be… a very special Halloween," Coral croaked.

April heaved both bags to the top of the stairs and looked up, surveying the old wooden hatch into the attic. She knew her dad wouldn't have forced his own sister – or stepsister, or half-sister, whatever she was – into there, so Coral really had *requested* the drafty, likely spider-filled if not completely infested, room. Wouldn't she die up there? April knew old people were less tolerant of cooler temperatures, and it was freezing up in the attic. How old was Aunt Coral, anyway? She couldn't be much older than April's dad, but something had aged her. Something terrible.

Sighing, April stretched up on her tiptoes and hammered a fist against the hatch. A wedge of blackness shunted open and she lurched up to grab the old ladder, yanking it down in one swift, if awkward, movement. The rungs plummeted down toward her on a squeaky old runner and she wrestled the ladder into position, making sure it was steady.

Satisfied, she returned to the bags, grabbing the snakeskin handbag first. It was easy enough to climb the ladder with it slung over the shoulder, and when she was halfway up she launched up an elbow to shift the displaced hatch completely out of the way, then she removed the handbag from her shoulder and tossed it half-heartedly up into the dark. There was a pleasing *thump*, and she slid down the ladder again.

What if Aunt Coral broke her leg getting up here? She was already walking with a cane, for Christ's sake. Another family disaster, April thought. Great. Just like Christmas '06. They'd spend Halloween night in hospital, and her father would declare the house permanently off-limits to family members.

That wouldn't be so bad. April almost found herself wishing that Aunt Coral *did* break a leg.

The duffel bag was unsurprisingly more difficult to heave up the ladder. She gripped all the straps in one hand, bundling them together and knotting them round her wrist, and climbed with the other. The heavy bag swung against her calves as she ascended, and halfway up to the hatch she almost fell. Finding a handhold above her, she pulled herself clumsily into the attic and with an enormous surge of energy she lifted the duffel bag in after her. It landed on her stomach as she rolled awkwardly onto her back, and she coughed in the dark, all the wind knocked out of her. Dust bloomed around her, clumps of pale particles dancing in the half-light filtering up from the landing.

Wheezing, her left arm aching as if she'd pulled a

muscle, April grunted and shoved the bag off her, stumbling to her feet. She looked around briefly; the attic was entirely dark, with no windows and only the faintest speckles of light from downstairs spangling the rafters. She moved carefully around the hatch toward a swinging, frayed cord the other side of the attic and pulled it sharply. The light came on after a few moments, buzzing as the filament warmed up and started to blare a dim amber.

Glancing down the hatch to make sure Aunt Coral hadn't followed her up, April felt a swell of vertigo – she was terrible with heights – as her eyes fell onto the empty staircase. No sign of the old woman, though she could still hear her heavy breathing coming from the kitchen.

April's dad had blown up an old camping mattress and laid three thick, folded blankets atop it with a spare pair of pillows and a sleeping bag for good measure. The ceiling was low and slanted and cobwebs hung from the beams, thick coats of dust clinging to them and turning them into ragged, dangling zombie fingers.

The duffel bag lay at her feet.

April looked out through the hatch again, cautiously this time. The staircase lilted away from her; still no sign of Coral.

April swallowed and returned her attention to the duffel bag.

She knelt beside it, one hand moving tentatively to

the zipper. The meat-and-decay smell had followed her up here, though she couldn't be sure that it wasn't just coating her clothes now like the clots of powder clinging to the cobwebs. She didn't know why she had such a sudden urge to poke her nose into Aunt Coral's belongings, but there was something about this bag. About the weight of it, the musty, ripe smell. The way something inside had seemed to slosh about as she lifted it up the ladder.

She pinched the zipper and tugged. The pungent smell worsened suddenly.

"Say... dearie?" came a sudden wheeze from right beneath her. April baulked, recoiling from the bag and whipping her head around to look down through the hatch. Aunt Coral was standing at the bottom of the ladder, one hand resting on the cane poked into the carpet, one gripping a rung halfway up so tightly that her knuckles poked up against the thin, almost translucent skin. Knuckles on top of knuckles on top of knuckles, rows and rows of them, like the gnarled roots of a tree which have folded in on themselves.

She can't see you. She can't see you.

So why was she smiling up into the attic so intensely? Why did the consuming, pinkish-whites of her eyes seem to be full of sharks suddenly, pools of pale ichor with miniature black fins poking up and circling, circling...

"Hey, Auntie. I was just—"

"Thank you… dearie. Would you… come and keep me… company?"

"Sure. Let me just climb down."

Aunt Coral stepped out of the way, apparently already attuned mentally to the layout of the landing – she avoided wheeling off the top of the stairs by a good foot and a half – and April climbed down. She hadn't heard Coral coming upstairs; hadn't imagined that the old woman could move *half* that fast. Now, though, as she descended the ladder, she realised that the ripe meat smell hadn't followed her up into the attic. It was here, where Aunt Coral was. It was her.

"So, Dad'll probably be home in half an hour or so," April said. "What do you want to do?"

"Mmm," Aunt Coral said thoughtfully, clasping her fingers into a tight knot around the head of her cane. "I don't suppose… you like toffee apples?"

April cringed. "I'm seventeen now, Auntie."

"Don't tell me… you've grown out of… sweet treats?" Coral's wrinkled face pinched in something that resembled dismay. The rheum of her eyes glistened.

"Sure," April said reluctantly. "I like sweets."

"Let's go make… some."

April blinked. "Make some?"

"It'll… be fun," Aunt Coral offered.

April exhaled. "Sure."

***

Her mobile phone rang as the boiling water was sucking the waxy skins off a bunch of Granny Smith apples in a large bowl on the kitchen counter. Aunt Coral had left her to watch over the apples while she went to the bathroom; April frowned confusedly at the unknown number and answered hesitantly, expecting a spam caller. "Hello?"

"Hi, sweetie," her dad said.

"Oh, hi Dad. Whose phone is this?"

"Pardon?"

"Somebody else's number came up. Are you borrowing someone's phone?"

"Oh… yes. Sorry. Mine died."

"What's up?"

"My tyre exploded on the way back from my meeting. I'm sorry, sweetie. Are you gonna be okay with your Auntie for a couple hours while I get this sorted?"

"You don't have a spare tyre?" April said.

"That was the spare tyre, hon. I'm sorry."

"Shit."

"Just my luck, huh? I'd walk back from the meeting hall, but clever me thought it'd be a great idea to drive to the petrol station for some sweets. Get a bucket of Celebrations or something for the kids tomorrow night. Tyre blew out three miles out of town."

"Halloween's on Wednesday, Dad," April grinned.

"Ah. Like I said, clever me. Anyway, I'll be home as soon as I can, all right?"

"All right."

"Love you."

"Love you too, Dad. Be safe."

He hung up, and April tucked the phone back into her pocket, returning to the bowl of boiling water. With a pasta spoon she scooped out a smooth, yellow apple and laid it gently on a tea towel on the counter. It smelled good. She dug the spoon back into the bowl and fished out another.

Upstairs, the toilet flushed.

The two of them sat in the living room and watched *Trick 'r Treat* as they ate a toffee apple each. April described the action for the old woman and ceased her narration whenever somebody on the screen spoke. She didn't think she was doing a great job, but the apple was delicious, and the film was a pleasantly fun surprise.

"Oh, now we're back with the werewolf girls," April said, her mouth full. "They're... well, I guess they're being all sexy. I won't go into detail."

Aunt Coral giggled, childlike, from the other end of the sofa. She had sunk into it and propped up her heels on Ron Leek's favourite footstool, the one built like a little four-legged sheep. She had already devoured a second toffee apple and seemed to be enjoying the film – or at least, the half-assed narration and the occasional screaming from the soundbar.

April side-eyed the old woman and smiled weakly. "You really like this time of year, don't you?"

Aunt Coral seemed to consider for a moment, then she nodded. "They say," she said slowly, her wet lips peeling back from teeth stained with brown sugar and vinegar, "Halloween night is the one night of the year when the veil between worlds is the thinnest. When the domains of the living and the dead collide."

Her wheeze seemed to have subsided somewhat. April figured it was just the fact that she was finally sitting down; poor woman must have been expending so much effort just to stand. April's gaze drifted to Coral's feet, and she saw that beneath the socks her toenails were long and curled, the toes themselves arthritically knotted together. The girl felt a sudden pang of guilt. Aunt Coral didn't have anyone to look after her; this might have been the only time of year when she even saw family.

"I've lost so many people, you know," Aunt Coral said quietly, staring blankly at the wall with her dead, mucus-covered eyes. "My parents. My husband. You wouldn't remember Alfie, though I think you met him once. You were just two or three years old, I'd say. Little chubby cheeks."

April swallowed.

"Little… chubby cheeks…"

It took April a second to realise that Aunt Coral had drifted off. Quietly she leaned over to the coffee table and fumbled with the remote, turning down the television until only the faintest horrified moans came out of the soundbar. Switching on the subtitles, she settled into the couch and watched the rest of the film.

When there was still no sign of her father by eleven, April decided she probably ought to get Aunt Coral to bed and get some sleep herself. Ron had probably found a hotel for the night somewhere just out of town and, being exhausted and stressed from his evening on the roadside, passed out as soon as he got to the room. That was why he hadn't called.

"Hey, Auntie," April said softly, shaking the old crone's shoulder. Coral's birdlike beak twitched and her eyes blinked open, her mouth snapping closed. "Time for bed, all right?"

Aunt Coral nodded, leaning forward. "I'm sorry," she said, laying a hand on April's cheek. The hand was ice-cold, the skin like leather. Something pulsed thickly beneath the flesh. "Would you help me upstairs?"

"Yeah. Are you sure you don't want the spare room?"

Aunt Coral smiled. "I'll be just fine," she said, her voice a little stronger than before.

April's father called again a little after that. April answered, relieved. "Hey, you okay?"

"I'm okay, sweetie. Sorry, it's been a hell of a night. I'll have to stay out here tonight and come back tomorrow, all right?"

"Can't you get a taxi?"

"More expensive than a night out, would you believe," her father said sourly. "And I'd only have to come back out here tomorrow to pick the car up. Are you and your aunt okay?"

"Yeah, we're fine. She's asleep. Did she really ask you specifically for the attic room?"

"What can I say? She's good friends with the woodworm."

"Weird woman."

"Yeah, well, the whole family can't be as normal as your dad, now, can they?"

April smiled. "Night, Dad. Let me know what happens tomorrow."

"Night, hon."

Placing the phone on her bedside table, April turned onto her side and stared at the wall. She could still hear Aunt Coral moving about above her; it sounded like she was pacing.

She struggled to remember why she had been afraid of the old woman. She was strange, a little eccentric – the pale-blue hearse that she'd arrived in was proof enough of that – and her eyes had creeped April out as a kid, but otherwise she was just a sweet, hunched-over lady. And she cooked a mean toffee apple.

April had fallen asleep within twenty minutes, the strange murmurs and sounds from the attic forgotten. She slept soundly, though her dreams were strange and feverish. She was waist-deep in water, struggling to wade across a wide, green river, when it froze around her. Became a great slab of ice, trapping her where she was. Still things moved beneath the surface, somehow flowing within the ice block, coiling around her legs—

She woke up cold. There was daylight. Broad strokes of it raked the window.

Begrudgingly, she tramped to the bathroom and prepared for college.

April leaned into the light, squinting at her reflection in the bathroom mirror.

Terror pumped through her blood and she froze.

There was a mark on her cheek, a hideous streak of blistered red in the shape of a long, dragging handprint. Its edges were the ochrous crimson of a birthmark, and it was dappled with pale spots like something diseased.

"Jesus," she hissed, reaching up to touch the dark

smudge on her face. It was crispy and striated against the pads of her fingers. It didn't hurt, but she was reluctant to rub or pick at it in case the layer of skin beneath was all blood. "What the hell?"

Then she remembered.

Aunt Coral's icy hand on her cheek, right where the mark was now. The mark that looked like a handprint.

Was she infectious?

Was *April* infectious, now that she had this thing?

No, surely not. It wasn't so bad, now that the energy-saving bulb had come on fully above her head and the light in the mirror was better. And it didn't look exactly like a handprint; what at first she had thought looked like long, rakish fingers were just streaks of slightly cracked skin. She had slept on a pillow that needed cleaning, that was all.

Shuddering with disgust, April opened the cupboard beneath the sink and fumbled inside for a tube of concealer.

She sat through ninety minutes of biology before breaking for an early lunch and deciding to skip the afternoon's chemistry class. She had wanted to be a doctor since before she could remember, always telling every grown-up that ever asked (and when you're a five-year-old, that's all of them) that she wanted to save lives. Recently she had discovered that chemistry was just about the most hideously complex thing one could voluntarily assign themselves to, and that biology was a close second. She liked the curly fries in the college canteen, though, and would often sit in there with her laptop and a coffee and research accounting courses and listen to historical lecturers waffle on about the Hapsburgs or whatever. There was something freeing about not knowing where her life was going; still, she resented the fact she'd wasted so much of it dead-set on a career that, it turned out, just… wasn't really for her.

She liked the idea of graphic design.

Who was she kidding? She'd probably end up in retail like everyone else she knew who'd left college and gone on to 'better things'. *Dreams are dumb and life is piss*, she thought, almost speaking aloud the mantra which had almost led her, in recent months, to ignore her father's warnings and jump into the deep end of a bottle.

Resisting the urge to scratch her face, April slammed the laptop shut and looked around. The canteen was decorated with thick orange streamers and orange-and-black paperchains. Glossy paper bats the size of textbooks had been slapped onto the walls and thick clumps of cotton-wool cobweb were draped across the corners and the doors and windows. There was murmured talk from across the room about some party at Tom Hecker's place tomorrow night. She wasn't interested. Tapping her foot anxiously, she surveyed the canteen tables for anyone she recognised and, not entirely sure whether she was disappointed or relieved that there was nobody she knew, looked up at the clock on the far wall. Almost ten to two, now. Still three hours to go till hockey. She had left a voicemail on the home telephone for Aunt Coral to let her know that she'd be home at six and that her dad would (hopefully) be home sooner, and told her to call if there were any problems or if she couldn't figure out the microwave. April wasn't desperate to get home, especially not if her dad was still holed up at a garage somewhere.

Increasingly restless, she slipped her laptop into her backpack and slugged the rest of her coffee (now cold) before heading out of the canteen and across campus. It was only a short walk into town and she figured she could head to the record store or something for an hour; why not, after all? It was that or sneaking into chemistry ten minutes late, and she knew how she'd rather spend her afternoon.

There wasn't much in the way of Halloween decoration around town, though three enormous crates of neglected pumpkins sat outside the Smart Discounts store with bright yellow sale signs plastered to the wood. A couple of the storefront windows were decked in orange and purple and a grinning, green-skinned witch cutout leered at her from the pet shop window.

The witch was holding a pure white rabbit in one hand and a sign reading "*Have a Hoppy Halloween!*" had been aggressively taped over the large, sacrificial knife in the other.

She looked left and right before crossing the street to the record shop – and paused as her eyes locked onto a dusty grey SUV parked on some double yellows a little way down the road. In the shadow of a row of terraced, redbrick houses, it was hard to tell at first, but as she walked cautiously toward it, it became obvious that it was her father's car. There was a shallow indent above the nearside headlight where he'd nose-bumped a bollard, and the rear window was smudged with a clot of birdshit that had dropped there a few days before. A couple of bright yellow parking tickets had been slapped onto the windscreen.

The tyres looked fine.

For a moment she feared the worst: what if somebody had done something to him? Dumped his car here on a side street, knowing that by the time it was found, it would be too late? But then she remembered that he'd called her, told her himself that the tyre had blown and he'd found a hotel for the night. He'd *lied* to her.

He was drinking again, she thought immediately, then she quickly cursed herself for assuming the worst. There had to be an explanation.

Reaching across the windscreen to check the

parking tickets, she fumbled blindly for her phone and dialled her dad's number quickly. When he didn't pick up, she dialled the unknown number that he'd called from the day before.

One of the tickets was from this afternoon. The other, October 29th. About an hour before April had come home from hockey practice.

Fuming, she waited while the phone rang, stepping aside as a red hatchback cruised slowly down the street. Pressing her back to the wall, she closed her eyes and listened. Two rings. Three. Four…

"The number you have called is not available right now. Please leave—"

April jabbed the End Call button furiously and shoved her phone back into her pocket.

There was something weird going on here, and she was determined to get to the bottom of it.

When she came home the ripe smell in the hallway was worse than before. It smelled like something had died and flopped limply onto the shoe rack, where its guts had spilled through the wooden piping into the carpet.

It was quiet.

"Dad?" April called, slinging her back to the floor. "Aunt Coral?"

Nothing.

"Dad!"

The house was silent, seemingly empty. She moved through the hallway to the living room's open door and glanced toward the landline sitting on the ottoman. The red light blinked up at her: Coral hadn't listened to her message. Didn't look like she'd even come downstairs. Had she been asleep all day?

"Oh, for fuck's sake," April snapped, scrambling for her phone. "Dad!"

She selected the unknown number from her recent calls and pressed the phone to her ear as she stepped back into the hallway and rounded toward the stairs. Christ, what if Aunt Coral had fallen over or something up there? What if…

"Pick up, pick up, pick up…" she whispered, climbing the stairs quickly. The hatch was closed and the ladder had been withdrawn into the attic. As she reached the landing she stretched up onto her tiptoes, preparing to knock with a tightly-balled fist. "Pick up…"

She froze.

She could hear ringing.

Slowly, she lowered the mobile from her ear and pressed it against her chest, muffling the dull dial tone. Her blood ran cold, her heart thumping loudly in her ears.

Above her: the shrill, tinny chirruping of another phone ringing. Somewhere in the attic.

April pulled back her arm like a spring, coiling it to

beat the attic door in. What the hell was going on? "Whatever this is, Dad, I'm—"

A shadow fell over her and she wheeled around, eyes widening in shock. Aunt Coral loomed between her cowering body and the top of the staircase, an enormous column of black-clad bone and thin, cracking flesh. She was dressed now in the black, lace cloak that had been hung on the coatstand – April hadn't even noticed it was gone when she'd come in – and it seemed to fold all the shadows of her body out into a billowing pyramid of pitch black ink. Aunt Coral laid both her bony hands on April's shoulders and smiled, flashing those thin, yellow teeth. Even through the material of April's shirt the woman's hands were icy cold.

"Auntie," April said quietly. The phone had stopped ringing. She tucked her mobile back into her pocket. "I didn't hear you come up."

"Oh, I was nearby," Aunt Coral said, her voice hardly cracking. She squeezed April's shoulders gently, then let them go. April noticed the cane with the carved, flapping birds was gone. "How was your day, dearie?"

"Fine. Did you hear a phone ringing up there?"

Aunt Coral glanced up with her blank, swimming eyes and shook her head. "It must be my mobile. Silly old me, I left it in my bag."

April nodded uneasily. "Right. It's just, it happened

to ring just as I was—"

"It *happened* to?" Aunt Coral said quietly.

"Well, yes, I suppose—"

"Oh, that reminds me," the old woman said cheerfully. "Your father called earlier. Said he'd fixed up his car all right, but he had to stay at work late tonight. Told me you'd be all right cooking dinner for us both?"

April paused. "Sure. Yeah, that's fine. Did he say when he'd be back?"

"Late."

"Okay. Can I just… did he call you on the phone you have in the attic?"

Aunt Coral smiled. "No, the landline, dearie," she said, "I imagine he was hoping to catch you, not me."

"Right."

"Would you like to come and carve pumpkins with me?"

April cocked an eyebrow. "What?"

"I bought pumpkins. I thought, since it's just the two of us again, we could—"

"Oh, I'm sorry. I'm not really into the whole… pumpkin thing."

Aunt Coral's eyes flashed brightly for a moment and April could almost have sworn that she glimpsed a tiny speck of black somewhere in the deep, gravy-like mess of each one. Disappointment pulled at the lines of her face. "Oh. That's a shame."

"But I'll do them with you," April said quickly, backtracking. "Why not? It'll be fun."

Aunt Coral smiled.

April led the old blind woman gently down the stairs, asking what she'd like to eat for dinner as she guided her carefully into the kitchen. As Coral spoke April only half-listened, shuddering at the thought of the cold, gloopy entrails of the pumpkin clinging to her forearm.

In a wedge of semi-darkness between the living room door and its frame, the red light of the untouched landline's answering machine blinked softly.

Despite everything April knew about Tom Hecker, she decided to go to his Halloween party.

His parents' house was packed to the walls with kids she knew from college. Weirdly, a lot of the kids from her high school were there too, but they were adults now. Strobe lights splashed the walls as a thumping bassline and the chorus of *Monster Mash* fought for control on the speakers. At first she thought it was nighttime, but when she moved to the pitch-black window she saw that a swarm of bats had surrounded the house and pressed their bloated, furry bodies against the glass in a mad scramble, wings batting at each other with a sound like rustling paper.

She turned wide-eyed back to the living room and

realised it wasn't Tom Hecker's place at all: this was *her* living room, and everyone was gone. All the party stuff was still there: red paper cups filled with green goop that she assumed was some weird Halloween flavour of chocolate milk; jelly with gummy eyeballs swimming around in it; candy bats and toffee apples and a barrel with blood bubbling in it. Was this what Halloween parties were like? She'd never cared for them.

She hurtled toward one wall and rummaged among a selection of bottles for one that screamed *I'm Your New Best Friend* and when she corked it and started to tip it into her throat the fire inside burned her on the way down. Suddenly everyone was back and the bats were inside. David Finch was there, directing. He pointed at her and said, in a voice that sounded just like her dad, "She's the one."

April stumbled out of the living room, shoving her way through a crowd of people she didn't know (though they all seemed to have faces that she recognised from some distant part of herself) and into the hallway. She had expected to see Tom Hecker shoving one of her college friends against the wall as he fumbled clumsily with his belt, but what she saw instead was Aunt Coral.

The music had died behind her and the only sound was the fluttering of bats' wings. When she looked back over her shoulder, the living room was empty again, but the floor was a black hole. David Finch was invisible, but she could also see him – only now he looked like Sheriff Harry Truman. He waved cheerfully, and his face exploded.

April screamed.

Thick, gnarled claws thrust into April's hair and twisted her head around, the bony fingers attached to them cold as ice and brittle like dead ash. Aunt Coral stood just inches from her, her vulture beak of a nose speckled with tiny dots of blood. Her pink-white eyes were swirled with streaks of gory red and her breath smelled like the repugnant, clammy tendrils of a pumpkin's insides.

When she opened her mouth, her voice was tinny and robotic. She said: "*The number you have called is not available.*" April tried to back away, but Aunt Coral had grabbed her jaw with the other hand and was wrestling it open, leaning forward to look inside her throat.

The rustling of bats' wings intensified and she moaned as more fingers poked into her mouth – and more, and more – until she couldn't breathe, and then Aunt Coral thrust her whole arm inside and reached down into April's chest and *pulled*—

***

Her eyes snapped open.

She felt fevered, her nose and throat blocked as if she'd suddenly caught a cold. Her whole body shuddered, but she was too hot. Boiling hot.

There were weird sounds above her head. A low, muffled chanting coming from the attic that sounded like guttural throat-singing. Scratching noises like something trying to scrabble through the floorboards.

April sobbed quietly, pulling the pillow over her head to blot out the noise. "Please," she whispered into the mattress, her voice suddenly weak and sickly. "Please, Dad, come home, please come home…"

When April crawled out of bed the next day her shoulders were sore. She peeled off her pyjama shirt and tipped her head to each side, saw that the pale flesh around her neck was bruised a dull blue. Reaching up to touch her face, she found that the skin of her cheek was blistered and felt like sandpaper. Something pulsed beneath the cracked handprint, like a little sac of warm fluid inside her face.

She bolted out of her room and down the landing, an uncontrollable shiver passing through her body as she dipped beneath the attic hatch. The house was cold and smelled like rotten fruit and dead animals. Tumbling down the stairs, April swiped her jacket from the coatstand in the hallway and slung it on, zipping it up to cover herself. She glanced frantically toward the front door, only now realising that both Aunt Coral's cloak and the wide-brimmed, black plague doctor hat were gone.

She had to get out. There was something wrong here, something horribly wrong, she had to—

She stumbled toward the door and yanked it open, her heart pounding.

It sunk into her stomach, deflated, as she saw a thick blossom of bright, burnt orange on the horizon. She shivered again, the evening air prickling her skin, her whole body trembling and feverish. Sweat dribbled down her back and made the insides of her thighs slick and cool.

Across the road, a bunch of trick-or-treaters were swarming number sixty-eight. Another, smaller group walked down the middle of the street, chaperoned by a girl that April vaguely recognised from college. Probably the older sister of one of the kids. Doors swung open and shut, cheerful middle-aged folks in dull cardigans offering sweets to the miniature ghouls and goblins that rocked up onto their doorsteps. At her feet, the two pumpkins she and Aunt Coral had carved – hers a sloppy mess that was meant to be some kind of Bigfoot, and her aunt's a surprisingly-detailed image of a man with long, stringy hair and two black holes for eyes – glowed yellow; somebody had taken the liberty of lighting them.

Somehow, April had slept through most of the day. Probably the fever – or maybe she hadn't gotten as much sleep over the last couple nights as she thought. Either way, she had missed college.

It was Halloween night.

April was about to step outside when the door slammed shut in her face, the waft of whooshing air punching her back a few steps. She wheeled around, immediately crashing into a tall, ice-cold pillar of shadow that had materialised in the hallway.

She pressed her back against the door, splaying her hands across the wood, and looked up into Aunt Coral's eyes.

"I didn't know if you'd ever wake up, dearie," Coral whispered, hunching forward so that her enormous beak of a nose was almost touching April's. The old woman's cloak was folded around her, the plague doctor's hat casting a wide, deep shadow over her face. Her mouth yawed into a wide, black smile, yellow needles bristling in her gums. She blinked, and the rheumy whirlpools of her eyes solidified, a sheen of glossy mucus slipping away to reveal two ink-black pupils, each one a tiny dot of shadow in a sea of fleshy nothing. Her smile stretched, the sallow bends of her face straightening as colour flushed in the caverns of her skin. "How about you join me for one... *last*... Halloween activity?"

***

The snakeskin handbag was empty. It lay opened and flat near the closed hatch, the black void of its insides spilling out into the shadows. Even with the flickering light on above them, the attic was only half-lit and the sickly amber peaks that crawled down the rafters only made it about halfway before retreating again.

From the handbag, Aunt Coral had produced a bone-handled knife, a slim box of matches, and a thick, leather-bound book with wrinkles in the cover so old they had formed a complex map of connected vein-like striations. This, she laid open on the surface of a small writing desk which she had pulled out from one corner of the attic. Sometime during her stay the air mattress had been deflated and shunted aside, and she had painted a titanic arcane symbol across the wooden slats of the floor. Glossy smears of bright, congealed red were twisted and knotted together into something like a circle, only it was broken in multiple places. Spears of bloody paint notched through the gaps shot into the edges of the room and up the walls, seven narrow pillars of crimson rocketing upward to converge in the middle of the slanted roof.

"What the hell is all this?" April moaned, watching in terror as her aunt hunched over the writing desk, dipping the handle of her knife into a small brass bowl filled with some kind of oily black ichor. Aunt Coral turned her head to smile back in April's direction, her eyes filled with some kind of sight that April didn't understand, didn't *want* to understand. Faint, folded wisps of smoke rose from the surface of the bowl as she stirred its contents.

"You don't remember your uncle Alfie, do you, dearie?" Aunt Coral said. Suddenly she seemed to stand even taller than before, her presence folded around a centre of mass large enough to suck all the gaps between April's individual heartbeats into its orbit. "My husband. My Alfred."

"I don't understand," April said, taking a step back. The hatch was open behind her. One more step, two, and she'd slip right through the hole and down the ladder—

There was a deafening *crack* as the hatch shot across the attic and ploughed neatly into the hole, shutting off all the light from below. April felt the whoosh of air as it moved past her and stumbled, looking down. A square of pitch-darkness sat in the midst of the red-painted carnage on the floor. Outside, the wind whistled fiercely. She could hear trick-or-treaters yelling, the pumping bass of a party nearby. They wouldn't be able to hear her.

"Please," April said, looking back in the crone's direction. Still hunched, still carrying that enormous cancerous burden between her shoulders, she towered over April, the smooth felt top of her hat pressed against the ceiling.

Aunt Coral's eyes narrowed. "I would like you to meet him now," she whispered, casting the little brass bowl forward.

A gluey clot of thin, black fluid splashed the floor with a searing sound like cold water on hot coal. April yelped as the whole house rumbled, the wooden slats trembling beneath her. Her head was already swimming and she staggered back as a wall of vertigo smashed into her, tumbling back into the rafters. Ripping her eyes off the floor she stared wildly in Aunt Coral's direction. "What the hell are you doing?" she shouted. Outside the shrieking of the wind had risen in volume and she could hear the faraway rumble of thunder.

"Tonight," Aunt Coral spat, her eyes alight, her needle-teeth twisted into a grimace, "Halloween night… the veil between our worlds is thin enough that you can *split it open*."

April's eyes dropped to the leatherbound book on the desk. On the open page she caught a glimpse of spidery, scrawled handwriting, oily red ink smudged into a miniature version of the enormous symbol painted on the floor. "Witchcraft," she whispered.

Aunt Coral smiled. The wide-brimmed hat tilted forward as she lowered her head, covering her eyes. April saw the cane in her hand and her breath hitched in her throat as she saw that the flapping swarm of birds carved into the wood were struggling, flapping their wings in a desperate and unhinged battle to stretch themselves out of the cane.

The old woman smashed the cane into the nearest wall and it exploded, splinters of wood billowing into the attic. "So many I have lost!" she screamed. "And all these years – learning… bargaining… I will see them again!"

"You're insane!" April yelled as a knot of shadows unfurled from the wall, dozens of sharp, bird-like shapes fluttering into the attic and dissipating. A splinter of light burst out of the newly-broken end of the cane and where it lanced the floor the wooden slats smouldered. April clamped a hand over her mouth to stifle a scream as the floor started to cave in, great chunks of wood falling away into a deep, black hole beneath. Her gaze shifted to the big black duffle bag and her heart shrivelled into a cowardly ball in her chest. "No…"

"I will see them again," Aunt Coral insisted, lurching forward and swiping a clawed, bony hand in April's direction. The girl ducked back, crying out as her head smashed the rafter and she tumbled to one side. "All I need is a little sacrifice…"

April leapt across the attic, staggering forward as the whole house shuddered beneath them. Outside the wind howled, screaming to be let in. She risked a cursory glance down into the yawing black pit that had opened up in the floor and thought she saw water rising from beneath, a great wall of ink-black water surging impossibly up toward them—

"You get back here!" hissed Aunt Coral, lunging at her again. She lashed forward with her bony fingers and raked April's back, gouging strips of flesh and leaving a hot bloom of pain spreading up the girl's spine. April screamed, falling onto the duffle bag.

"Is he in here?!" she yelled, fumbling with the zip. "Did you put him in here, you sick old bag?!"

Narrow fingers clenched around April's throat. The skin blistered instantly, searing as if the ice-cold hand was covered in a glove of liquid nitrogen. April yowled, tipping her head back. Aunt Coral's blinding white eyes beamed down into her and the old woman opened her mouth. "I think I'll have to stay in this hotel for one more night, *dearie*," she snarled, and her voice wasn't her voice anymore. It was a perfect replica of Ron Leek's, right down to the intricate inflections of his speech pattern. Aunt Coral grinned. Using Stacey Hipperson's voice now, she said, "Why don't you open the bag?"

April blinked away tears, the house rumbling so loud she thought it might crumble around them. "This is insane. Why would you do this? Did you kill him?"

Aunt Coral seemed to soften, crouching down before her. The broken cane in one hand, she twisted her fingers into April's hair and blinked. "I need two," she whispered. Behind her, the sound of gushing water. Lapping the broken floorboards. "One dead. One alive."

"Why us? We're family," April moaned. "We're your family…"

"It didn't have to be you," Aunt Coral shrugged. "It just had to be tonight. But since I was here…"

"You're sick," April sobbed. "You're sick. We're *family!*"

Aunt Coral looked back toward the yawning black pit in the floor. April followed her line of sight and saw that the ragged hole had filled with water, black as tar, and now it was bubbling, boiling furiously. "So are they," Aunt Coral whispered, and she yanked April to her feet.

April struggled against her but Coral was too strong, shoving her toward the water's edge. The house had stopped shaking but the water was still rising, spilling over the slats and lapping her feet.

"Sit," Aunt Coral snapped, shoving April onto her knees so that she was close enough to see her reflection in the oily surface. White smoke hissed across the water, fog obscuring the reversed image of her face. Behind her, the old woman retreated to the duffle bag and zipped it open.

April sobbed into her chest as Coral returned to her side and tossed something into the water. There was a splash as if something the size of a basketball had broken the surface and April couldn't help but look, ripping her eyes from the floor to glance across the ink-black lake—

Her father's eyes disappeared under the surface. The fog had begun to climb, forming spiralling pillars that lurched up toward the ceiling. Some of them had started to form shapes, almost-human shapes, and they stood on the surface, translucent and bloated, waiting, reaching...

"No," April moaned, turning her head to look back toward the duffle bag. Ron Leek's headless body spilled out of it, elbows and knees broken, limbs folded in on themselves. The bones poked out through his flesh, huge chunks of him missing, the stump of his neck ragged and red. "No..."

"Now for your part," Aunt Coral whispered, and something cold and sharp snicked April's cheek.

April screamed as blood gushed from the swilling sac in her face, the blistered mark on her cheek rupturing open and gluey rattails of bright red viscera pouring out and spilling across her teeth. Aunt Coral's hands were in her hair again and the old woman shoved her head forward, grunting excitedly. April's blood trickled into the water and the girl watched in terror as streaks of crimson shot forward, bubbling beneath the surface, rising, rising—

April staggered to her feet and shot an elbow into space; miraculously it smashed into Aunt Coral's chin and the old woman stumbled back, groaning as her teeth ground together. Before she could think April had hobbled past the open duffle bag, her sights set on the writing desk and the ancient-looking leatherbound book. "Tell me how to undo this!" she yelled, scrambling for the book.

"You think you could handle any of the spells in there?" Aunt Coral screeched. "Even if you had magic in you, child, those incantations are beyond your capabilities!"

April grimaced, looking past Coral into the attic. The foggy humanesque shapes on the surface of the bubbling lake had started to twitch and convulse, thick knots of blood rising from the water at their feet and coiling around their limbs. Blood fused and knitted into bulbous shapes and strips of meaty red and striated muscle. She glanced down at the book, panicking. Started to turn the pages, scrambling desperately for an answer. Much of the writing was in Latin but some was made up of arcane symbols she couldn't begin to understand; some was illustrated with figures of the devil, of demons. "Magic book," she whispered. "Magic book, come on…"

"Fool!" Aunt Coral roared, lunging forward and snatching at the book. April ducked out of her reach and stumbled across the attic, almost toppling into the water. "To think you could reverse this—"

"I don't have to," April realised. She looked up into

Aunt Coral's eyes and grinned. "It's like a textbook, right? Like a college textbook for witches. And if there's one thing I know about college textbooks—"

She fumbled through the pages, ducking another swipe and crashing into the writing desk.

"—it's that the easy shit is right at the front," she finished, turning to the first page and reading aloud. "*Hunch miser in parvae*—"

"No!" Aunt Coral yelled.

"—*magnitudinis creaturam convertam!*"

There was a sound like a whipcrack, then an intense bubbling. Heat filled the room and April looked desperately up from the book to see the blood-bound creatures straddling the lakewater thrashing frantically as they began to sink down beneath the surface. Whatever awful magic Coral had used to bring them up from their wretched plane of existence, something had gotten in the way of it.

She looked across to where Aunt Coral had been standing.

Her eyes dropped to the floor.

"You're shitting me," she said.

The snake was a king cobra, its scales patterned in strips of pale cream and slick, oily black. Its squat, beady-eyed head was framed by a majestic hood of splayed snake ribs. Its teeth were pointed, yellow needles.

April toppled back as the snake darted forward, lashing its venomous tongue at her face. The book tumbled from her hands and she rolled to one side, splinters printing into her skin from the rough, wooden floor. The cobra lunged forward again, neck snapping toward April's gut—

She reached out with both hands and grabbed the thing by the neck, squeezing hard. Its tail whipped up and smacked her arm but she ignored the bright bolt of pain, rolling over again to pin the creature to the floorboards. "Fuck you!" she yelled. "I don't care what night it is, fuck you and fuck off!"

Slamming the creature's head into the writing desk, she grabbed its tail and pulled.

April stood in the kitchen and sighed.

Gripping the cobra tight by its head, she stepped up to the freezer and wrestled it open with a trembling arm. Grimacing, she opened the top drawer and carefully removed a bag of frozen peas, a cheese-and-tomato pizza, and half a loaf of bread.

The cobra twitched in her hand as she worked.

***

For a while she sat in the hallway in absolute silence, hugging her knees to her chest and rocking back and forth. She had cried for an hour now.

The attic door was closed – she would make sure she found some way of *keeping* it closed some point soon – and it was over. Finally over. Just a few more hours, and Halloween itself would die in the sunlight.

A knock at the door made her blood run cold.

She stiffened. Looked up, steeling herself.

This was it, she thought. She'd known *somebody* would call them.

Straightening her legs, April heaved herself to her feet and brushed down her jacket. She took a deep breath, let it out, and walked up to the front door. Here it comes, she thought. The barrage of blue lights, the officers on the doorstep at the end of every crap horror film.

Swinging it open, she said bluntly, "I'll come quietly, I'll tell you anything you want to know. And if you don't believe me, Aunt Coral's in the freez...er..."

Three kids in Halloween costumes stood on the doorstep. Two mummies and Batman.

"Uhh," Batman said, "trick or treat?"

Relief flooded April's chest. She almost crumpled to her knees right there. Laying a hand on her chest, she said, "Sure. How about a toffee apple each?"

Behind her, the freezer hummed peacefully.

Author's Note:

A prequel! If you've already read my novella Parliament of Witches, *then you might have had an idea what you were in for the moment you saw the title for this story. But this story, incidentally, was written long before* Witches. *In fact, when the concept of a green-amber-red collection first began to develop into one that crossed a colourful 'spectrum' of horror, I thought it would be fun to take the colours-for-titles theme I was running with and work with a colour that could have been a name: hence 'Coral'. The character of Aunt Coral was born and quickly became something truly hideous, which was tone down quite remarkably for the story itself. The novella followed, and the rest is – actually, that's about it. There isn't really a 'rest' of it.*

AMBER

He arrived a little before dark. They'd called him in the early hours with the news and a location, and he'd left his car in the small lot at the edge of the marsh as instructed. For miles, he had slogged through clumps of grass and dips and valleys in the rich, clay soil. His clothes were stained brown and yellow with the paste-like sludge he had tramped through.

Huxley Dean was starved, exhausted, desperate for a drink, and quite certain that this could not be the place.

The house had been described to him, but he couldn't quite believe the state of it. The wooden slats were crooked and dark with damp, the greasy windows smeared with soot. A strange light glinted on the roof of the rotting building, an iridescent kaleidoscope of pink and gold turning over itself in the slow sunset.

Dean stood in the cool shadow of the house and gazed up at the glassy shimmer of light. From here he could only suppose that perhaps some obscene metal or glass structure, jutting from all the chewed-up ends of the wooden pieces making up this skeletal, two-storey hut, might reflect the last of the sunlight in such a way.

There was a small hand-axe dug into the wooden slats of the porch. Stepping past it, he knocked on the woodworm-eaten door and pressed it open. It screamed as he entered.

"Hello?" Dean called, wiping his boots on a ragged doormat and moving into a sparse, narrow entrance hall. He shrugged off a heavy, waterproof rucksack, leaving it beside the door. Ahead of him and to the right, a rutting staircase ground its way up the wall towards a bony landing. On his left, an open doorway led into a small kitchen. Another beside it was closed and padlocked. "Hello, I'm here for the job? I was told somebody would... be here..."

Nothing. Nobody.

Briefly, Dean's hand moved to his stubbled throat. Three days he had gone without a drink, but still he craved it. He'd been told it would become easier. That each day would bring its own challenges, but that he would learn to overcome them.

That each day would become shorter, in time.

He longed for those short days. For now, he was confused and mildly infuriated and he wanted, more than anything, a double measure of Jameson's to numb the throbbing in his head.

No, he thought, moving through the hallway to

explore beneath the stairs. A small alcove had been dug out from the husk of the staircase, and was filled almost to waist-height with hunks of roughly chopped wood and three pails of coal briquettes. Beside him, a slender metal chain with a sooty pearl handle hung from a rusted lever in the wall.

A small package had been nailed to the back of the door. Reaching up for it, he carefully tore open the paper and found inside a wedge of cash totalling two hundred pounds – his wages for the first night – bound in an iron wallet clip; a curried beef sandwich and bottle of water; and a note in a small, square envelope.

Fumbling to open it, he heard a crackle. The pop and whistle of burning wood, coming from above him.

Silently, Dean slid the note into the pocket of his corduroys and backed toward the stairs. The steps moaned beneath him; the whole cabin seemed to tremor and shift in the loam as he shambled through it.

"Hello?" he called, reaching the landing. He pushed open the first door on his left and saw the makings of a small bedroom: a single mattress on a rusted metal frame; a knotted writing desk and a window overlooking the marsh, through which he could see a thick, black gash of forest on the horizon where some monstrous hand had clawed the trees from the landscape.

Behind the second door stood a urinal and small washbasin. And at the end of the landing, a narrow, black ladder peeled up the wall toward a trapdoor in the ceiling.

He listened, gazing up at the trapdoor. And after a moment, flickering beads of orange begun to drip through gaps between the slats, and he heard the crackling again.

"Christ," he hissed, running for the ladder and hauling himself onto it. Already he could feel the heat from above; he heaved himself to the top of the ladder. The trapdoor opened with some effort and he thrust his body through, overcome with an intense wash of heat as he scrambled onto the stone floor above.

He stood, bending to accommodate a low glass ceiling. Firelight throbbed and pulsated around him as he looked about the room, bewildered.

At the very top of the house, a glass dome overlooked the marsh. Huxley Dean stood on a gritty, concrete ring, in the centre of which an enormous stone bowl screamed with flames: logs wheezed and whistled in a shallow vat of shimmering fluid. Fire licked at the glass, slipping through slim vents between the polygonal panes that made up the dome. Thick, black smoke rolled out and filled the night sky, and shifting, orange tongues of lanternlight were cast out into the marshlands.

"What are you—"

"Do you know your job?" came the flat voice of a bald, naked man standing beside the bowl. He was impossibly thin, his scrawny frame bulging where angular, bird-like bones pressed against the skin. His skin was covered in something slick and oily that shimmered in the firelight and made the bird-man look like some insane, grinning spirit. When Dean didn't answer, he repeated: "Do you know your *job*?"

"Keep the lamp lit," Dean said dumbly, echoing the instructions he'd been given. "What—"

The naked man stepped forward and tipped into the bowl.

The mucus-like fluid covering him lit immediately and his whole body erupted into a rabid, sprawling madness of flame before he'd completely folded into the basin. His bony body fell inward and his head tilted back as thick tongues of fire coiled around him, surging up his throat. There was a *whoomph* and heat surged through the dome, running down the glass panels like rain. Dean yelled and staggered back, eyes flickering to the glass as an explosive wash of amber blossomed out of the dome and through the dark. There was a piercing wail from outside – the wind? – and a wall of shadow seemed to shunt back into the night, as if pushed violently away from the house.

Before he had time to do anything else, he saw that the bird-man's skin had begun to boil away. He was screaming – or perhaps Dean was, and it had all mixed together – and his scrawny arms flailed as the fire consumed him. Pulp exploded from blisters across the man's back and his eyes ran down his face like jelly.

Then he was gone, slipping into the bowl and deeper into the fire and screaming all the way, and Huxley Dean was left with the flame and the image of the dead man's grinning face burned into his brain.

The dome was intensely warm, but for most of the night Dean shivered. He sat beside the trapdoor, as far from the flaming bowl as possible without leaving the strange room altogether. He hugged his knees, rocking a little as the grotesque scene played over and over in his head. He had considered running, but he would never find his car all the way out there in the dark. The marsh would have him.

Besides, he had a feeling that the task he'd been given was more profoundly important than he'd imagined.

Do you know your job?

Dean thought that perhaps he didn't. If he looked toward the bowl, he could still see that clawed, blackened hand thrusting out of the flame, flesh slowly dripping from the reaching bones of the bird-man's fingers. He looked around instead, his eyes darting feverishly about the room. Sweat poured down his face and matted his hair.

Beside the bowl was a small stack of logs, some drenched with fluid. Across the other side of the concrete walkway ringing the firepit, he saw a discarded bottle. Wide, clear, and empty. The markings on the label had been burned away, but he knew the smell of alcohol. He had smelled it on the naked man. He smelled it now, spilling into the dome as flames splashed the ceiling and smoke oozed through the vents.

He looked away, turning his attention to the glass.

The marsh was a vast, crashing expanse of tall grass and tumbling inlets, scarred horribly by the trenches and ponds that scattered its surface. Everything was lit in flickering shades of lamplight; even the thick, dark black of the night was not enough to combat the dappled glare of the fire, amplified and magnified as it was by the prisms of glass all around him. There was something different, he thought, about the glass itself: each pane seemed to swell and wane in the centre as though warped, almost pearlescent in its transparency. Designed and arranged specifically to spread that light across the wetlands as efficiently as possible.

Outside, he saw massive pillars of shadow. In the distance, four of them rose from the grasses around the forest, disappearing into the dark of the night above before he could make out their shape. But he saw more, spread around the marsh, surrounding the awful house, surrounding *him*.

The adrenaline coursing through him had begun to fade. His limbs were exhausted, his brain wracked with fear.

After hours of sitting, moveless, in the smouldering heat of the firepit, he finally fell asleep.

Dean woke with a start. Cold swam through his bones and he jolted upright, smacking the back of his head on a warm glass panel. His eyes moved to the bowl and widened as he saw that the flames had died back, that the fire was now little more than a built-up pile of embers and ash.

"Shit," he murmured, coughing as a bitter swill of smoke clawed hungrily at his windpipe. He stumbled up and to the bowl, reaching for a pair of logs by his feet.

He flung them into the bowl, ignoring the charred bones sticking out from beneath little rippling dunes of ash. The flame caught them instantly and reared up its head; dipping back from the sudden wash of heat, Dean tossed in two more hunks of wood.

White, electric energy soared around the edges of the dome and filtered out once again to cover the marsh in a thick blanket of firelight. Dean turned, looking out through the glass.

His heart stopped.

The pillars of shadow rising from the marsh had grown closer. They were absolutely still, but they were no longer at the very edges where the grassland met the forest. Now they swelled from the clay soil and thrust up into the night, each one only half a mile or so from the cabin.

And while he still could not make out their shape in its entirety, he was acutely aware that they must have one. They had moved in pairs, it seemed.

Like legs.

Eventually the dark simmered back and pink bands of soft light scraped the horizon; day came, and the shadows outside disappeared as the fire in the bowl went out for good. Dean waited a while longer, and then he opened the trapdoor and slipped down the ladder, desperate to relieve himself. His head pounded; before, he would simply have opened a bottle and begun his day by calming that dull throb to a whisper. Now, though, he was stronger than that. This was his fourth day sober, and he was determined to make five. A week, even.

That was a part of the reason he had taken this job: to be – for a while at least – away from it all. Isolated, alone, unable to steal quickly to the shops or the bar for a pint.

Just he and his thoughts, a night shift to keep his mind occupied, and not a drop to drink.

After visiting the grotty bathroom on the upper floor, he moved downstairs and to the kitchen to find food. In the latter hours of the morning, he had decided, he would run. The marsh would be easy enough to traverse in daylight; his own footsteps, even, might still be there from the night before, sunk deep into the muck and mire. Yes, he would be all right then; he would get away from here and forget about the whole thing.

Opening the kitchen cupboards, he found rum.

Dean slammed the first set of doors and moved to the next cupboard. Inside it, he found more. The bottles were aged, clear and round and wide like the empty one he'd seen upstairs. The rum inside was as transparent as the glass that housed it. Eighty-five proof. Each bottle was sealed with a cork, but still the smell of ethanol stung him.

The cupboard beneath the sink was filled, too, with more bottles. Dozens on each shelf, packed tightly. Even a small cool box was filled with them.

"Jesus," he moaned, moving back into the hallway as he ran his hands through his hair. Turning, he saw that another package had been nailed to the front door.

Someone had been here.

He remembered the note. Patted his pockets and found it tucked into his cords. Unfolding it, he read quickly, his vision hazy with exhaustion:

"The house guards from The Dark."

He tore the second package from the door. Inside, he found a curried beef sandwich, a can of beans and another wedge of cash.

If They reach it, They will cross over.

He swallowed, moving nervously to the wood store beneath the stairs as he scanned the scrawled handwriting. *Light keeps Them still*, it read. *At night, if allowed to, They will move.*

He looked; not enough wood, he thought. He had seen how quickly the lantern burned down.

Rum burns better than blood.

But blood – enough blood, all at once – will send Them back to the edge.

Dean shook his head. This wasn't happening. "Jesus *shitting* Christ," he whispered.

He folded the note into his pocket and moved to the rucksack he'd left by the door. Changing quickly, he scratched at the frayed, rough stubble of his chin and opened the front door to step outside.

He bent down, wrenched the hand-axe from its place in the wood of the porch, and started off toward the forest.

This was someone else's problem, he thought as he waded across the marsh. Evidently someone had come to the house this morning, and it seemed likely they'd be able to find another sap to man the lamp at night – after all, *he'd* been desperate enough to do it.

He was, however, not without a conscience, and so he had elected to chop enough wood for his successor's first night. He'd found a discarded barrow around the back of the house and knew it would take a few trips to fill the wood store, but it would keep his mind off the copious supply of rum in the kitchen and the desperate need for it in his belly.

Dean reached the woods and trudged into the dark between the trees. A little way in, he found a felled ash and began to hack at it, generating a small pile of pale logs in a little over an hour. Loading up the barrow, he turned it around to cross the bleak wasteland back to the house, then paused, deciding to look a little deeper in the woods for more storm-felled trunks. If there were none around here, he might have to find another patch of forest.

Arms sore, Dean ventured into the woods.

He froze at the sight of a dark figure between the trees, the size and shape of a man. He supposed that was what it was. And another, standing just a few feet to the right of the first. Another on his left. Dean turned his head and looked.

A row of them. Standing in the dark, their eyes on him. Or they might have been, at least, but he couldn't see their eyes for the tight, black masks they wore.

Not just a line, he realised, turning his whole body to peer into the trees, but a circle surrounding him.

They were dressed all in black—black robes, black waistcoats, black trousers and thick, black funeral dresses—and each one had a tar-smeared burlap mask pulled over their face. As one, they raised their right hands and pointed.

Behind him, the way he'd come. A clear gesture: *go back*.

He understood, then, that they'd already taken his car.

Night came, and he kept watch of the lantern. He packed it early with firewood that he'd dragged or thrown up the ladder, and by the time it was fully dark the fire was blazing bright.

He ate quickly and poured rum into the bowl to keep the light flaring thickly through the glass. Holding those bottles was like repeatedly taking a gun, loading it and pointing it up into his throat; he was tempted to pull the trigger, but the fear of what might happen if he let the flame go out kept him from squeezing.

Dean curled up at the edge of the dome and kept his face sheltered from the fire. He considered the rum again. Looking up to see how much was left, he noticed a pearl handle on the opposite wall, similar to the one hanging from the chain downstairs. He stood and moved around the bowl, ignoring the sick, wet pop of the burning logs. Ducking beneath a cloying ribbon of smoke and examining the pearl handle, he saw that it seemed to operate the entire framework of the dome; that pulling it would twist each iron bar in such a way that slender shutters peeled across the glass and blotted out the light.

His hand moved slowly for the switch and he tugged it gently. There was an awful screech as the shutters closed – glass scraping glass, a sound like rasping breath through a tin whistle – and for a moment the marsh was hidden from him behind a wall of dreadful, drunken black.

He tugged the handle again and the shutters opened.

Outside, the pillars of shadow had closed in. The light had only been out for a moment – the blink of an eye – but they had come thirty or forty feet in that time. A dozen pairs of huge, shadowy legs taking enormous strides toward him, blocking the moonlight in every direction.

Another few seconds, he thought, and the dark
(*the Dark*)
might have reached the house.

Dean grabbed more logs and threw them onto the fire before heading downstairs to get another load.

Over the next few days, Dean developed a routine: picking up the day's wages and food from the package nailed to the door, he would eat quickly and sleep for three or four hours before heading outside and collecting wood in the afternoon. Dragging the wood back to the house and all the way up to the glass dome on the roof was a chore, and chopping and gathering enough material for the night took him until dinnertime, at which point he would eat a little more before heading up to keep watch for the night.

Already he could feel the weight dropping off him; the rations kept him going, but were not nearly enough to sustain him. But the real damage was in his head: the desire to drink chipped away at him, and the crippling temptation of the endless supply of rum in the kitchen was enough to drive him mad. His skin was badly burned, and he had begun to experience a dry, regular coughing. Presumably, he had swallowed a lot of smoke.

But the worst thing was the watching. It was enough to drive anyone insane. He wondered, ferrying barrowloads of wood to the house, whether it had done so already.

He remembered the man who'd passed him the torch – quite literally – on that first night.

If he wanted

(*enough blood*)

to give up, to pass on the job to someone else

(*all at once*)

would he have to make

(*will send Them back*)

the same sacrifice?

They wouldn't let him leave any other way, he was certain enough of that. Should never have taken the damn job. Should never have answered the damn *phone*. And the moment that poor bastard threw himself into the fire, he should have *run*.

He returned, most days, to the locked door beneath the staircase.

He toyed with the padlock, trying to ease the door from its frame and peer into the crack. He could see nothing. But they were hiding something from him in there, he was sure. Something else.

At night, he stood by the glass and watched the shadows on the marsh, trying to discern their shapes, their faces. But where each pair of huge, ink-black legs met at what might have been a waist, the shapes melted into the dark of the night above and became nothing. The marsh below was splashed with amber and gold, the stalks of brittle plants swaying in the wind and making it all look like some ethereal shining ocean.

Feverish, maddened by exhaustion and fear, he returned on the sixth day to the locked door. He had barely carried half of the wood he'd need for the night into the house, but he thought he might collapse with exhaustion. He had ventured farther into the forest, found another felled tree – the hooded figures had stepped aside to let him hack at it, but he had seen a blunt knife in the hand of one, thought he might have glimpsed a similar weapon in the hand of another.

They weren't letting him go any further than that.

Barely thinking, he ploughed his boot into the

padlock and the flimsy bolt shattered. The door exploded inwards and he tumbled through into a small, low-lit room.

The ceiling slanted beneath the weight of the stairs above. The walls were lined with narrow, crooked bookshelves, and upon them more rum. Dozens and dozens of bottles, some half-drunk. He had gone for almost a full week now without a drop – more than he'd managed in a long time, and he wondered if that was partly responsible for everything he'd been seeing – but he was… god, he was thirsty. One day at a time, he reminded himself, one

(*dark*)

day at a time.

He prayed for shorter days.

There was a dead man sitting at a tiny writing desk in the middle of the room.

All around him were sketches of tall, thin shapes, shapes with impossibly long arms and legs and without faces or eyes. Dark, shadowy shapes. Drawings of men and women in black burlap masks. One appeared to wield a flat butcher's cleaver; another a hatchet of some kind.

The cleaver from the picture was buried in the dead man's forehead, and his brains – spilled down his face – had long since dried. There were no flies, and he did not smell. His skin was badly burned, and coated in a thin layer of sticky, transparent viscera, but it was certainly the cleaver that had killed him.

They had *meant* for him to break down the door, Dean realised. To find this.

It was a warning.

There was a note pinned to the cadaver's chest. *Only when you feel you can keep the lamp lit no longer*, it read, *ring the bell. Another will come.*

"Ring the bell," Dean murmured. "What bell?"

He stepped back out into the hall and looked up, toward the chain hanging against the wall. The chain with the pearl handle. Slowly, he went to it. Gingerly reached for the handle. The pads of his fingers brushed smooth, cool marble. He gripped it, considered.

No. He couldn't do it. Couldn't put someone else through this shit.

Not yet.

And not if it meant throwing himself into the fire like his predecessor had done.

Glancing toward the open front door, he saw that it was getting dark.

Dean curled into a knot by the wall and let the fire burn. He had removed his shirt and sweated steadily, hot mixing with cold where his bare back pressed against the glass. Outside, the shadows stood where they had for days, tall pillars of black looming like stone sentinels, surrounding him. Every now and then he tossed another log onto the fire. He had brought some of the rum up with him and he doused each chunk of wood first; the flames burned strong and thick and yellow, casting amber pillows of light out through the polygonal glass panes.

Exhaustion throbbed through him and his head nodded forward, lolling heavy on a neck that had given up trying to support it. His arms and legs were stiff. His chest pulsed weakly and slowly, his breathing frail. And there was something clawing at the back of his skull, wriggling around in there, something like lunacy. And he was *tired*. Numb and weak and tired; Christ, he was so fucking

his eyes opened

the fire was roaring and his head nodded forward again and a weight fell across his face and his eyelids

yelled as he snapped awake and through bleary eyes saw the shadows outside, reaching, still, and the ribbons of flame were still thick and raging and he bobbed forward and

elbow smacked the glass as he

and then he was awake, properly awake, and the fire was out.

He blinked furiously, wincing as his neck and back cracked loudly. The flames had died and the ashes smouldered a deep, wet orange that rippled in the bowl.

"Shit," he murmured, "shit, fucking shit *shit*—"

He fumbled for the woodpile with shaking hands, his whole body cracking and popping like the burnt-out fire. His fingers scratched at empty space. He wheeled around, ignoring the shadows outside, reaching desperately for a log that wasn't there—

"*Shit.*"

He scrambled to his feet and reached for the nearest bottle of rum, tossing it into the bowl. Clear fluid splashed the smouldering embers and for the smallest split second he was terrified the liquid might put it out for good, then a *whoomph* of flame shot up and he felt the heat slide wetly across his face, felt the skin burn over his cheeks and forehead, felt his eyes well up with smoke. He looked up, saw nothing but black through the windows of the dome – but now the yellow firelight beat at it, batting it away…

Not enough.

Dean lurched across the room and to the trapdoor, almost falling through it. He climbed down quickly, tumbled onto the landing; moving through the empty house like a demon, he ran for the front door, knowing he must have left some of the wood out there, knowing there'd be *something* he could burn—

He opened the door and looked up into the dark.

It towered over him, a mountain of monstrous shadow. The colossal thing stood barely twenty yards from the rotting house, a gargantuan beast without a face. Its legs were impossibly long and its arms bent forward, reaching for the dome with massive fingers as if to stamp out the light that had frozen it into stillness. It was a statue without skin, almost human in shape but indescribably dark, and it made Dean's blood run cold enough that he forgot the agony of the burned, blistered flesh of his face.

He grabbed an armful of wood from the pile on the doorstep and hurried back inside.

Huxley Dean didn't leave the dome until the murky, grey morning light had fully settled across the marsh, and even then he left the fire lit. He broke his usual routine: didn't sleep in the morning, just went out to the forest to gather wood. A lot of it. In seconds – for he was sure he could not have been asleep for longer – they had moved close enough to reach out and grab the house. One more slip like that, and he'd have failed. And why did he care? What was it about the house that they wanted? What was it he was there to protect?

The thought crossed his mind briefly that the house was some kind of decoy, that there was nothing there at all but that the Dark had been convinced otherwise. Or perhaps there was something underground, something buried beneath the foundations; he didn't think he would find out.

Enough blood, all at once, will send Them back.

That was why the narrow man had thrown himself into the fire on his first night, he knew. To give Dean a head-start. He had known that the hooded figures in the forest wouldn't let him leave, and chosen the easy way out. But in doing so, he had somehow reset the shadow-monsters' progress across the marsh, sending them back to the horizon; the blast of fire released through the glass when his blood began to burn had hit them all at once and shunted them away.

Dean wondered how close those dark giants had been before that.

When he'd gathered enough wood for the night – and a little more – Dean stood in the hallway of the old, empty cabin and stared at the pull handle. A sliver of marbled pearl dangling from a crusty chain. Perhaps it could end all this…

And you'll die, he reminded himself. His shoulders and back ached from carting wood across the marsh and from sitting all night in that awful glass chamber. Either he would summon somebody new and throw himself onto the fire as… as what? A gesture of goodwill? or he would run, and they'd kill him.

Either way, it was better than this.

His whole body tore at him, his mind slowly ripping itself to pieces. He was burned and burned out, exhausted beyond repair, and above all that terrified of the things out there in the marsh. Though they had disappeared, again, in the daylight, he knew that tonight they would return and that the closest one, the one that had drawn right up to the house, would be close enough to touch…

What happened, then, when he fell asleep again? Even for a second, for a moment…

There was no choice. He'd failed, and he had to send Them back.

Enough blood, all at once…

Time to wave the white flag, he thought. Time to admit defeat and call in the cavalry. He steeled himself, reached up, and pulled the chain.

As the marsh began to darken, Dean lit the fire in the dome and watched through the window. The shadows appeared all at once with the last pink light of the sunset: one close enough to grab the dome and rip it from the roof of this awful little cabin, and another, if he turned to look in the other direction, bent over and thrusting its shadowy fist into the back of the house. More still would reach him if allowed another step. Amber washed their faceless faces and painted their shadowy forms in rippling, selfless gold, streams of red and white-pink darting between thick fingers and roaring up enormous arms to their shapeless, smooth heads. The house was a gateway, and if they were allowed to pass through…

Below him, the front door creaked open.

Dean bent down and reached for a half-empty bottle of rum. The rest had gone on the fire. He glanced down into the bowl; swirls of orange and blue ploughed up into the whirling mix of light that splashed the windows.

Someone called out from the hallway. "Hello? Is anyone here? I've come for the—"

Dean swallowed. "Up here!" he called. His throat was full of smoke, his lungs shrivelled with it.

He waited. Footsteps on the wooden landing. A pause. Then a hand clapped onto the metal rung of the ladder, and another. Dean turned.

A slender figure crawled through the hatch and into the dome. A woman of thirty-odd, her hair pulled back into a bun. Her neck and hands were scattered with deep, red blotches. Her eyes were dark and wet with confusion. She looked at him.

Dean crossed the chamber and held out his hand for the woman to shake. She took it gingerly. "What is this?" she said.

"I wish I'd been able to ask that question when I started," Dean said quietly. He moved toward the fire, keeping his eyes off the windows, and the woman did the same. "I'll do you a courtesy that my predecessor never afforded me. See, this job would be so much easier if you just… knew what you were getting into."

"What am I getting into?" the woman asked hesitantly.

Dean pointed to the glass. "Do you see them?"

The woman turned. He heard her gasp, saw her put a hand over her mouth. "How did I... good god, I just walked right through the middle of them..."

"Enough blood, all at once," Dean said, "will send Them back."

The woman looked at him, frowning. "Wha—"

Dean swung the bottle of rum and smashed it into her jaw. The glass shattered and clear fluid sprayed her face as she tumbled back, her neck snapping with an audible *crack*. Dean stepped forward and caught her, one hand on the small of her back, the other gripping the broken bottle neck. "I'm sorry," he whispered. "I don't want to do this."

The woman's eyes widened.

He thrust the bottle neck forward and slid the jagged lip of it into her throat. Glass pierced flesh and muscle easily and he tipped her back, wincing as a steady stream of blood poured from her throat and into the fire. Behind him, the shadows of the night flickered. The woman gargled, red bubbles frothing at her lips.

Dean dropped her and stepped back. She screamed – half-screamed, her throat red and glossy and in ribbons – as her skin began to blister. The fire had consumed her before she could fight or flail, before she could stand and scramble out of the bowl. Dean stood with his back to the glass and watched as the flames ripped at her and her flesh began to boil and bubble, long, melted strings of it sizzling as they oozed into the bowl. Fire poured out of her mouth and her eyes burst with the heat, swilling in their sockets like badly-poached eggs.

He turned and watched as a thick, sweet wave of lamplight poured out onto the marsh and smacked at the dark. There was no sound, no ceremony, but all at once the gargantuan pillars of darkness surrounding him were shunted back, slipped back into the night, and he was alone.

So alone.

Dean picked up another discarded bottle from the floor and sat, defeated, with his sweating back pressed against the glass.

He wept. For a long time – almost until morning came and the light burnt out – he wept. He gripped the bottle for hours, watching the fire until the poor woman's bones had turned to curled, black shafts of brittle nothing in the bowl.

Then the fire died, and Dean stood up. He went downstairs. There was a package tacked to the door. Inside, the night's wages, a curried beef sandwich, and a bottle of water.

He stood in the hall for a long time, considering the pearl handle of the chain. Not yet. No, he would try again; do better this time, keep them away for longer.

The less he had to ring that bell, the better.

Dean unscrewed the cap of the bottle, took a long, deep drink, and prayed for longer days.

Author's Note:

Like I said in my introduction, this is perhaps one of the first – if not the *first – horror stories I ever wrote. Certainly it has gone through a couple of redrafts in the last few years, but this story was the foundation for my love of writing horror and one of the things I've clung to since its creation. Now, finally, it's out there. Out here, I should say. And I hope you liked it.*

Beware the Marsh Lights, and pray for longer days.

Thank you for reading.

Thank you for reading *Marsh Lights*. As an independent author every single person reading my work is so valued and I can't express how much your time means to me. For more of my books, follow me on Instagram @heath_horrorwriter or check out my website derekheathhorror.com where I'll keep you updated on future releases.

I hope you enjoyed! If so, please leave a review on Amazon if you can. I'd love to know what you thought.

ALSO AVAILABLE FROM THE AUTHOR

Day of the Mummy
Night of the Bunny
Dark Nights (Stories)
Dead Engines (Horror Stories of the Railway)
Moondisc
Empire of Cold
Endless Living Organ Massacre
Drop Bear (Outback Terror: Book One)
Parliament of Witches
Burrow

Milton Keynes UK
Ingram Content Group UK Ltd.
UKHW021633260524
443160UK00001B/4

9 781915 272751